THREE ROAD

ALSO BY EMMA TIMPANY

Novella

Travelling in the Dark (Fairlight Books, 2018)

Short Stories

Cornish Short Stories: A Collection of Contemporary Cornish Writing
(co-editor, The History Press, 2018).
The Lost of Syros (Cultured Llama Press, 2015)
Over the Dam (Red Squirrel Press, 2015).

THREE ROADS

& Other Stories

EMMA TIMPANY

First published in 2022 by Postbox Press,
the literary fiction imprint of Red Squirrel Press
36 Elphinstone Crescent
Biggar
South Lanarkshire
ML12 6GU
www.redsquirelpress.com

Edited by Colin Will

Layout, design and typesetting by Gerry Cambridge
gerry.cambridge@btinternet.com

Cover image painted by Adam Drouet

Copyright © Emma Timpany 2022

Emma Timpany has asserted her right to be identified as the author of this work in accordance with Section 77 of the Copyright, Designs and Patents Act 1988.
All rights reserved.

A CIP catalogue record for this book is available from the British Library.

ISBN: 978 1 913632 34 2

Red Squirrel Press and Postbox Press are committed to a sustainable future. This publication is printed in the UK by Imprint Digital using Forest Stewardship Council certified paper.
www.digital.imprint.co.uk

Trivial *adj*. 1, of small value and importance...
(Latin, = place where three roads meet
(as TRI-, *via* 'road'.)

The hardest thing of all to see is what is really there.

—J. A. Baker, *The Peregrine*.

Contents

Stars • 11
The Rememberer • 17
Three Roads • 23
Impressionism • 35
Shepherd's Bush Blues • 41
Peregian • 49
Par Temps de Pluie • 57
Girls on Motorbikes • 61
A Bird So Rare • 69
Over the Dam • 77
Like Leaves • 85
La Crue de la Seine • 99
Error • 101
Tissue • 109
Flowers • 111

Notes • 134
Acknowledgements • 136
A NOTE ON THE TYPES • 138

For Adam, Iris and Lauren, with all my love.

* Stars *

ONLY AN HOUR LEFT until you arrive. I've filled a roasting tray with sweet potato, red onion, courgettes, added rosemary-infused oil, dotted on some olives, sprinkled on some thyme. The wine stands open breathing on the dresser. The table's laid with best white linen and in a line along the centre I've placed every candle I can find. When the lights are out and the candles lit, we'll be afloat in our own galaxy, the cloth a Milky Way of countless stars, the candles and the cutlery our white and silver points of light.

Forget the first of January. Today is the true midwinter, the day of longest darkness, the moment when the balance shifts and light begins its slow return.

You'll laugh when you see this table. It's unusual for me to go to so much trouble, to be this organised. I can be when it really matters. I've spent the weeks of your absence doing all the things I said I'd do but hadn't. So much rests on this one meal. Fifteen years of everything. You promised you'd come back and eat with me tonight. You said it would be the final time. You made me promise not to beg or plead, and I agreed.

So this is it. My last attempt to tell you what *you* mean: to tell you why you must not go but stay with me. Many times I've tried, and many times I've failed. Fifty minutes is all that I have left.

Remember the day we met, high on that Dorset hillside? The day of the solar eclipse—three celestial bodies in a row—a syzygy of earth and moon and sun. The moment the sun was lost, there came a vast cold. The dogs began to howl, the most heartbroken, desolate wailing

I've ever heard animals make, and then it started, this bitter wind. I've never forgotten it, the cold that came. I've never forgotten the howling.

It's only a few moments, you said, but I'd swear even now that time was different then. And then you smiled and said, *Isn't it great?*

Already I was thinking, *So this is what it will be like...* and that song started in my head, about the stars going out one by one.

My aunt used to play that song on hot nights in Brisbane. I'd fold myself into the big black leather chair, the one her husband left behind when he left her, along with the record player and the records and the things that I could never get over, the silver shields belonging to his dead first wife, trophies for the long ago races she'd won. There were dozens of them, nailed to the wall at the side of the bar under fluorescent bulbs which bathed everything in weird, blue light. That chair was big and black, and I was still small enough to curl up in it. The air outside the open windows was warm and soft, and the song played in the darkness, and my aunt said that some nights she'd drive out to the airport and park by the fence alongside the runway and spend hours watching the planes take off. It was too dark to read the names that were written on their silver bodies, but she'd watch them and wonder where they were going and whether, one day, she'd go to those places too, and the sad voice in the song would sing something about flying away and then I couldn't stand it anymore, the leather hot and soft and fleshy like a black throat about to swallow me.

These last few days I've been feeling that way again, like I've been sent alone on the plane to my aunt's house, unaccompanied minor, the tag tied around my neck. On those journeys I'd be thinking, *Why am I here? I want to go home now. Why can't I go home?* Except that this time it's *you* I want to come home. I want you to come back.

I don't understand how all these moments live inside me, one on top of the other. I mean, how can they, really, all fit inside one head? It's only forty years' worth of stuff. What's going to happen when I'm, say, I don't know, ninety? It's not as if the thoughts go away. They lurk and then pop out. They unfold like some complicated bit of paper or an old list you've written on this way and that and have to squint at to decipher.

Now I'm thinking about the time we were driving up that valley, by the river whose name means white destroyer. On the gravel between its threaded waterways, on the banks between the channels, were tree trunks gnawed pale by its force, and the water was dark from the leaves from the forests. Huge boulders, square as dice, lay scattered on the valley floor as if they'd fallen out of a monster's pocket. I'd promised to take you to the waterfall. The glaciers were creaking, and the waterfall fell from so high up that by the time it hit the ground the water had wafted sideways, even though there was no wind to speak of. We tramped through fields followed by herds of scary cows. When we reached the pool, we stripped naked and jumped in. The water was so clear we could see the white stones shining on the bottom, but when we tried to dive down, we realised it was an illusion and the pool was massively deep. The cold made our scalps contract, and my skin felt as if it were burning, burning. You left your watch there, on those grey rock slabs, but we didn't realise that until later.

Where I come from, at midwinter, stars appear, low in the sky, riding the tail of the Milky Way. As the stars rise, we call out the names of those we've lost in the year since they last set. These stars are young, so young they dwell in the dust and gas they were born in. Still, they understand our tears. After we've shared our sorrows, we open our oven doors so that the smell of good food cooking can strengthen them for they are cold and weak.

That's what I'll do as soon as your headlights sweep the drive. Onions will be sweetening, sweet potato softening, the spikes of rosemary for remembrance crisping, all of it touched by the wild scent of thyme. The scent will warm you, draw you in.

Last year at Brù na Boinne, remember? You held my hand in the inner chamber, older than the pyramids. No rain had reached that place for five thousand years. Only now do I understand it, know why the Neolithic farmers built those odd stone structures lined up with the last mid-winter light. They knew all about the cold of the gone sun, knew, no matter how momentary its absence, the fear of times when the light is so dim it might have been extinguished, the years when the rain is ash.

That's what it's like when your face turns away from me. The coldness of the end of time blows in on that strange wind. Animals begin their lost howling. I'm curled up on that chair again, living in a house with a dead woman's trophies on the wall. I'm driving to the airport in the dark and watching plane after plane take off into the black.

What I'm trying to say is *go no further from me*. It's time to shake off that cloak of stars, wipe the moon's lipstick off your shoulder, and come back.

I know what their lives are, the women who've lost love. I've heard them outside in the darkness, beneath our windows; the rustling and quivering of their silks and satins at parties, their sad lace stretching over breasts and hips, the texts from them you glance at, half-smilingly, barely read, quickly delete. When you're talking to them, back turned to me, I see it on their faces—desire, fear, need—but most of all a craving for your light. They launch their ships for you, paint their pictures for you. In you, they catch a glimpse of their one true home. By the time they smell their city burning, you've already gone, stepping lightly across the grasslands and the plains where, for one like you, a river might rise up and speak and fight.

You and your strange associations, you said, the first time you put your arm around me, pulled me close. *There's no one else would put these things together.* You leant forward, touched my cheek. *No one else would ever think that we could be as one.*

In a moment I'll hear the car. The first beams from your headlights will reach my waiting house.

Let's go back to the waterfall. It's the kind of place where the right gesture, well-meant, might confer on us immortality. That watch of yours was good quality, its battery supposed to last a thousand years. The next time I won't lose heart. No matter how chill the water, no matter how deep the pool. No matter how much the cold burns my skin or the pressure pushes the air from my lungs, I won't give up. I'll dive right to the bottom of that clear water, over and over and over. I'll grab fistfuls of those white stones we once saw shining there and, while you lie back on hot, grey rocks, I'll cover you with stars.

* The Rememberer *

THE REMEMBERER WAS SMALLER than she had expected him to be. He was on the short side, with all that that entails for man's pride, in his mid to late fifties maybe, his squirrel grey hair cut to a fuzz, his eyes a weird shade of blackish blue. His face spoke of a life lived out of doors, possibly of time spent at sea, or perhaps just plain hard living which had robbed it of any softness. Sand-coloured chinos; a short-sleeved shirt from Marks & Spencer, checked cotton, not new but well ironed; a pair of worn but highly polished chestnut brown shoes on his feet. He sat forward in his chair, elbows resting on spread knees, hands clasped and tilted so they pointed in her direction. He did not smile. He was silent, with that listening type of silence that indicated that he was waiting for her to begin, his eyes fixed firmly but not aggressively on her as she slid into the seat opposite him and placed her oversized bag on the floor at her feet.

'The first thing I need you to remember is that my daughter needs to finish her birthday thank-you cards. And then she needs to practise her piano pieces for her exam next week. She needs to write the birthday card for tomorrow's party tonight and pack a change of clothes because she's going to the party straight after school. And remember to remind me to tell her not to go kayaking if she's not sure what she's doing. Or if it's not a sit-on kayak. And I need you to remember the names of the plumber's children, and the plumber's name, too, and to tell my husband that the accountant needs *all* of his bank statements. And that the credit card statement for last April is missing, presumed drowned. I need you to remember that the children now need sun cream on in the morning, and I need you to remember to check whether they've brushed their teeth after breakfast. I need you to make sure that they do their homework; this week it's an entry for the local garden show, some decorated cupcakes, or a garden on a plate. I need you to remember to tell the builder that the delivery is going to be late; also, the plants in the greenhouse need watering and for the next five mornings the bird feeders need filling because my husband, who usually does it, is away. You need to remind me to text my sister-in-law to say thanks for the photos of the puppy but that I couldn't open them on my phone so could she please email them instead? And to remember to text her my email address in case she doesn't have it. And to chase up my husband about finding his nephew's address in Canada so I can post the thank you cards we wrote for the photos they sent. And remind me to send the subscription renewal to the magazine which has been lost for a year but turned up when I was looking for the missing bank statement. You need to remember that my *belle soeur* is babysitting tomorrow night and will need to be fed so after dropping the kids at school tomorrow I need to remember to pick up some mince from the farm butcher because it's in the same direction and while I'm down there to remember about the birthday party because there is a lane, apparently, just around that bend, from where I will need to pick my daughter up and after I've got the mince you need to remind me to go to the shop because we're out of cheese, can you believe it, and mushrooms and courgettes and pasta even though we buy those enormous three kilogram bags of the stuff that look as though they could never run out. And that it's Thursday so I need to remember to get the local paper because there is likely to be a picture of the kids in it. And remind me to tell the kids that Aunty is babysitting tomorrow so not to eat too many sweets and to brush their teeth really well because they know what the dentist said last time. And to tell the little one that I love her and to sleep tight because she'll be in bed before I get home. And to tell the big one that I love her too, even though she'll be awake when I get home, so she doesn't get hurt feelings. And to ask my husband if he wants to eat before or after the meeting. Or to just find out what time he's getting home. And if he's got everything he needs to go away on Friday so there aren't any last minute panics. And remember to check if he's got the train tickets and the Oyster Card for the tube. And to allow enough time to park the car, not like last time. And remember that I need to take the girls shopping for their father's birthday presents over the weekend, and to buy more wrapping paper and to make time to think about what he might actually like for his birthday. And remember that a few days after that it is also our wedding anniversary, and while I am shopping, I need to remember that my younger daughter has two birthday parties coming up one of which clashes with a swimming lesson, so I need to remember to ask the swimming teacher whether it matters if my daughter misses the penultimate lesson.

Did I mention wrapping paper?

The multi-use boy/girl/adult/birthday/any occasion kind and lots of it. And to remember that the builders need their mugs, cleaned overnight in the dishwater, taken out by 10am for their morning cuppa. And that I must remember to collect them later, along with the rubbish bins and the recycling boxes. And remember I need to look again for that ball of string which I know is somewhere because my daughter wants it to finish the car seat she's making for her favourite stuffed toy, a tiger, out of a cardboard box. And remind me to remind my older daughter about her fingernails. And that she needs to ring her best friend about meeting up on Saturday. And ahem, can you remind me,' I felt a little bashful at this point but his calm, intense expression put me at ease, 'to wax my legs this evening because the weather is supposed to get better this weekend. It's turning golden, apparently. After all this rain. And I keep forgetting to do it.'

I paused to take a breath. The Rememberer gave what might have been a slight nod.

'Okay?' I said.

He didn't reply but made the same slight head movement again. I wondered what his name was and whether he had a family.

'What's your name?' I said.

'Jeremy,' he said.

I couldn't place the accent, but that was something I was useless at anyway. 'Is that okay, Jeremy?'

'Yes,' he said, 'that's fine. Is that all?'

'For now,' I said. 'Same time tomorrow?'

'Later,' he said. 'Two p.m. tomorrow. Same place.'

'Should I go now?'

'Yes,' he said.

Outside, unlocking my car, I felt much calmer. I had been worried that something was wrong with me, perhaps a brain tumour or something similar, because lately I have had these lapses. These forgettings. Great chunks of stuff, of time itself, had disappeared from my mind, for example much of what I had learnt at school, until I began to wonder whether I *had* learnt anything at school. The same with university. It had got better for a while in my twenties but then, in the aftermath of children and a five year stretch of intense stress, it had happened again. At times, my speech was also affected. A muddling of words, of ideas, occurred. I began to wonder whether it would ever be reversible or whether, this time, at the age of forty-two, I had travelled too far to get back to what I once had been: a person who could remember things. Hence the attempt at redress. Hence engaging the services of the Rememberer.

He remembered everything for me for all of that day and, when we had a quick catch up call late in the evening, we were both pleased with the results. Nothing had been missed. But early the next morning came the first lapse. I had dropped the children at school and was heading in the wrong direction when my mobile rang. I found a place to pull over and took the call.

'Mince,' he said, in a black-blue voice.

'Of course,' I said. 'I'll turn back.'

And once he had said 'mince' I remembered to look out for the lane I had not been down before, the lane I did not know, at the very end of which was a house where the children's party would be held. I drove up the lane I did know through the beautiful avenue of beech trees, touched as ever by its deep green soothe, and parked outside the butchery. On a lawn a peacock stood with its back to me, tail spread in a fan. After killing the engine, I sat and watched it. I could not remember the last time I had seen a peacock with so stunning a tail on display. I will stop for a moment, I thought, and enjoy this. Who knows when I might see its like again?

The back of the fan was black and white, beautiful in its monochrome way; at its base was a soft bed of fluffy white feathers, a touch of glossy blue on its sides and beneath those lay five or so long, soft goldy-bronze, finger-like feathers curving inwards like a baseball mitt, seeming to act as a counterweight to the great fan trembling above them. Nearby a peahen stalked, pecking, her head close to the ground, her feathers, warm grey and white, lying close to her back, seemingly unimpressed. The peacock turned and shook his eyes at her, and I noticed something I had not seen before, tall, spear-like feathers, perhaps new or half formed, pointed, eyeless, which spread through the purple and indigo screen. I watched as he strutted and shimmied and shook. I watched her ignore him, passing him by six or perhaps seven times, and then, when she moved between him and the low hedge, he tipped his fan forward like a net and covered her, climbing her back, his tail settling over them like a glorious coverlet. A minute, perhaps less, went by and then, shaking herself free of him, she went back to pecking. I thought he would put his tail down for good then, but to my surprise he kept it up. To what purpose, I wondered, now that the deed was done?

I have lingered too long, I told myself. I need to get out of the car now and go through that doorway and buy mince. Organic, local, delicious mince to feed all these people of mine. For all I know that peacock will keep his tail up all day. It is time for me to get going.

By the time I left the shop he was settled on the grass, his fan folded. My disappointment was so great that, for a moment, before turning on the ignition, I let my head flop back against the rest. When I closed my eyes, I found the sight I'd witnessed had stayed with me, in fine and glowing detail, and that I had a perfect memory of the things I had just seen.

* Three Roads *

THE EDGE OF A MEAT PIE, peeping out from white paper bag spotted with transparent blobs of grease, dangled loosely from Sissy's hand. The buttery, wheaty smell of hot pastry was usually appetising, but today her side throbbed with a dull, blunt pain which only eased when she bent forward from her waist. She dropped the pie in the bin and held her side while sipping water from a stainless-steel fountain. Nica, her sister, was seated amongst a group of girls high up on the grass, a ghetto blaster in their midst playing Midnight Oil.

Today was a half day. School was over for the term, but they were not going home; their mother was away at a conference, so Sissy and Nica were staying with family friends for the weekend. The Meer's house was almost enclosed by a circular barrier of beautiful trees: a lawn ran from the front steps straight towards the harbour, giving the impression that if you ran to the end of the grass and jumped, you would land in the water.

At dinner time, Sissy picked at her rice, eating it grain by grain, while Ralph, the Meer's dog, a grey-pelted, yellow-eyed creature, went to sleep on her feet. The next morning, the pain in Sissy's side felt much the same. Breakfast held no allure. Out of habit she pecked at some toast and sipped some coffee. Nica and Sissy were supposed to help Mr Meer paint the dining room, transforming it from a dim green, an interior outpost of the trees, to a fresher, lighter cream. Sissy started opening the tins of paint with a knife blade. A transparent shiny layer of oily stuff had congealed on top of the paint; her task was to mix it back into a smooth solution with a piece of doweling, ready to be poured into trays. The smell of emulsion was nauseating, but Sissy carried on. If she faltered she might well be accused of laziness, of shirking.

At morning teatime, Mr Meer made mugs of milky coffee and handed around a jar of broken chocolate biscuits; the chocolate was covered in white patches where the milk solids had separated from the cocoa.

'It's okay. They're still perfectly edible. Would you like one?' He shook the jar a little.

'No, thanks,' Sissy said.

'That's not like you,' Nica snorted. 'You're normally a pig when it comes to chocolate.'

'You were off your food last night as well. What is it, Sissy? Not feeling well?' Mr Meer's hand was too big to fit into the jar. He shook a fragment of digestive into his palm.

'Not really.'

'Would you like to lie down for an hour?'

'Yes,' she said, avoiding Nica's glare. 'I would.'

The spare bedroom was in an attic space. On the wooden walls hung tapestries of meadows, castles, white unicorns with downcast eyes. Mrs Meer returned from her squash game, swiftly mounting the stairs, impatient to get on with whatever she should have been doing. Although Sissy did not yet have periods, Mrs Meer diagnosed period pain and made Sissy hold a hot water bottle. Sissy's body was beginning to reshape itself. It was no longer possible to stand upright and even in bed with her knees pulled up, the dull pain kept tightening her abdomen.

After another hour had passed, Mr Meer came into

the attic room and put his hand on her forehead. 'I wonder what's wrong with you?'

He seemed to be waiting for an answer to his question, so Sissy said, 'I don't know.'

Moments after he left the room, muffled shouting echoed up the stairwell.

'Her mother needs some time to herself,' Mrs Meer was yelling. 'Ring the doctor if you want, but I'm not having Amanda miss her weekend away.'

Mr Meer's voice was very quiet. Sissy couldn't hear his reply.

'If she's putting this on to get attention, I'm going to tear her to shreds,' Mrs Meer screamed. 'With my bare hands. Don't you *dare* shush me. I don't *care* if she hears me. To *shreds*.'

Sissy lay on the backseat and Ralph, who usually had to go in a wire cage in the boot, was allowed to lie in the foot well. When the car began to move, she locked eyes with him. After they had looked at each other for a while, she felt increasingly certain that Ralph understood everything. The sickness had started to seep out of her, forcing from her pores a strange, wrong, metallic scent. She was no longer herself, not quite, and the dog knew it. She could feel the dog's sympathy very strongly, and the doctor's too, because although he smiled a great deal and talked in a very loud voice as though she were deaf, it did not take him long to say, 'It's straight to the hospital with you, I'm afraid. We won't wait for an ambulance. It'll be quicker if Simon drives you there.'

But at the hospital once the nurse had taken her arm and she was lying on a trolley bed, Mr Meer—Simon—said that he had to go. He said that he'd get Nica and that they would come back to the hospital together and then, after speaking to the nurse, he left her.

Not long after that Sissy threw up green bile in a bowl made of moulded cardboard. Afterwards she lay on her side with her knees pulled as far towards her chest as possible. The doctor had a beard and a small gold sleeper in his right ear.

'Where's your mother?'

'My mother's away.'

'What about your father?'

'He died.'

'Oh. I'm sorry. Who brought you here?'

'Friend of the family. Mr Meer,' one of the nurses said. 'He's gone to get her sister.'

'How old are you?'

'Thirteen.'

'How old is your sister?'

'Fifteen. I'm going to be... sorry.'

'Don't worry about that, Sissy. We can clean the floor. Your appendix is extremely enlarged. It may have already started to burst. What time did she come in?'

'Four-thirty.' The nurse looked at a message on her pager. 'The sister's here.'

Along with her sister came the smell of too strong an application of Lou-Lou. Nica's lashes shimmered purple with the expensive French mascara she'd shoplifted from Kendall's that smelt of violets. Her eyes were ringed with kohl, her permed hair kept back, Madonna-style, with a piece of ragged lace, and her fingernails glimmered witchily with acid green polish.

'So where are the Mars family? Mr Mars? Mrs Mars?'

Nica looked at him blankly.

'These people looking after you while your mother is away?'

'The Meers. They dropped me off outside.' Nica popped some gum.

'By yourself?'

'Yep.' Nica rolled her eyes.

'And why did they do that?' the doctor said.

'They had a dinner party to go to.'

'Did they leave a contact telephone number?'

Nica shrugged. 'Doubt it.'

The doctor squeezed Sissy's hand. 'Don't you worry. I'll make sure you're all right.'

'Name? Parents' names? Address? Medical history?' the nurse said. 'Ever had heart disease, kidney problems, liver problems, diabetes? Anything at all?'

'She's had ringworm,' Nica snarled. 'Does that count?'

'Stroke? Asthma? Eczema? High blood pressure? Cardiac arrest? Breathing difficulties? Any sexually transmitted diseases?'

'Look at her. Can't you *smell* the virginity?'

'Let's get your watch off, Susan. I'll put it into this bag with your name on it.'

'Nobody calls her Susan.'

'So, who do we call in the event that...you...she doesn't...Do either of you know where your mother is staying?'

'Nope.'

The nurse gave a deep sigh. 'Religion?'

'Catholic. Sort of.' Nica spat a wad of yellow gum into a grizzled tissue.

'How can you be *sort of* Catholic?'

'Our parents were different religions. We were supposed to decide for ourselves when we grew up.' Nica's favourite vocal style was the monotone; it drove their mother wild.

'Shall I get Father Davidson for you?'

'I wouldn't bother.'

'You don't have any idea how serious this is, do you? I'll see if there's time before your sister goes in.'

An orderly grabbed the trolley and started pushing Sissy's bed. The nurse trotted alongside, and Nica sloped along the corridor, arms crossed tightly across her chest.

They travelled upwards in a huge elevator. When the doors opened, Sissy saw a man in green baggy clothes standing with his back pressed to a swing door, holding it open. Inside the room were bags of clear fluid on stands and two more men in green gowns, who smiled brightly at Sissy and chatted with a great deal of animation, as if she were a friend that they had been longing to see and they were all at some kind of immensely enjoyable party. The nurse held out her clipboard in front of Nica like a barrier. 'You can't go any further. Sign here. And here. And here. And here. And print your name. And sign again here. And here. And here. This is it. Time to say goodbye.'

'Somebody bring me a bucket because I'm gonna spew,' Nica screamed as the door swung closed.

When Sissy woke up it was night. Dim artificial light pulsed beyond an open doorway. She was wearing a blue gown made of the same thick, stiff cotton as a tablecloth. A white sheet was pulled up over her as high as her chest. Her bones felt as though they were made of something heavy, stone perhaps, or concrete. In fact, the heaviness was all through her and, for some moments of sheer terror, she thought she could no longer move. Something huge and dry filled her mouth. Slowly and with difficulty she moved it, realising the wretched swollen mass was her tongue. With each tiny movement moisture came, until, after a phase of deeply unpleasant stickiness, her tongue worked loose. Her throat was so dry it was painful to swallow, and she felt a great and terrible thirst.

Her arms trembled as she lifted the sheet and gown and looked at her lower body. A sticky strip of something that looked like mucky Sellotape held two bits of her skin above her right hip together. On the bottom sheet, also near her right hip, was a large stain and she wondered whether she had somehow wet the bed. She reached down and dabbed her fingertips into something dark and sticky, a sizable patch of still damp blood.

A nurse stood in the doorway, looking into the room, the light behind her so that only her outline showed. Sissy had not heard the nurse coming because she wore those shoes that made no sound, soft-soled and purest white like her grandmother's bowling shoes. The nurse came over to the bed and looked at her and did not smile.

'You pressed your buzzer.'

'No.' Because of the dryness, her words came with difficulty.

'Yes, you did. Look.' From underneath Sissy's body, the nurse pulled free a remote-control shaped object with a long, curly, telephone cord tail. 'Are you in pain?'

'Thirsty. Water.'

'You can't. You're nil by mouth.'

She thought the nurse would go away but she stayed near the bed, looking, from time to time, at Sissy's face. After a while, the nurse said,

'Are you sure you're not in pain?'

'Not in pain. Very thirsty.'

The nurse looked again at her chart. 'Unusual surname. Your father was in hospital a while ago, wasn't he?'

'Yes,' Sissy said eventually.

'How is he?'

Sissy shook her heavy head.

The nurse did not say sorry. She was the only person who had not said sorry.

The nurse said, 'I suppose I could see if you can have some ice.'

Ice was one of the last things. Her mother and uncle had spooned ice into her father's mouth after he turned yellow and his bed was moved into the front room. There were four last things and one of them was ice and another was cold flannels on the forehead and the injections the doctor gave and there was one other thing, but she could not remember what it was.

'Tears are a good thing.' The nurse sat on the edge of the bed. 'Don't try to stop them.'

After a few weeks, or perhaps it was a month, Sissy was allowed to leave the hospital and go home. She was not well enough to return to school, so her teachers sent her classwork home with Nica. In the mornings and sometimes later in the afternoons, Sissy sat up in bed and tried to study.

Amongst her work was a series of Level One Latin books about the lives of two freeborn Roman girls. Around their necks, Claudia and Flavia wore heart-shaped amulets called *bullae* containing objects to ward off evil. This custom, the notes explained, was a tradition that the Romans had taken over from the Etruscans because, during their early years, children were seen as especially vulnerable and in need of protection from evil spirits, witchcraft and harm of other sorts. When girls were betrothed or married, they would take off their *bullae* and dedicate them to Trivia, goddess of the crossroads. Sissy realised, even with her fledgling understanding of Latin, that *Trivia* meant 'three roads'.

Years later, after gaining her degree and graduating, Sissy found work overseas, and moved from country to country to make the most of her life. Now she was in her thirties, her new friends and the people she worked with called her Susan. It was only when she returned to the place that she was born and grew up in for a week once a year that she became Sissy again.

It had never been easy to find things to talk to her mother about. Often there were long silences between them.

'For some reason I was thinking about the time I had my appendix out,' Sissy said one morning. 'But I don't remember how long I was in hospital for. Was it one week? Two?' On Sissy's stomach only a faint silvery line, a slight thickening of the skin, showed that her scar had ever existed at all.

'You were in hospital for four weeks. Don't you remember?' Long ago, Amanda had told Sissy and Nica not to call her Mum; she felt it aged her. 'Once you came home from the hospital, it was at least six weeks before you were able to go back to school.'

As with much of her adolescence, when Sissy tried to recall it, she felt a curious blankness. She remembered the bearded doctor who tended to wave his hands around while he was speaking. He'd made her two promises and failed to deliver on one of them: to bring her partially burst appendix in a jar to keep as a memento. The other promise he kept. He visited her every day, even when he wasn't on duty, his ears burning when the nurses teased him about it. The nurses all blurred into one, apart from the nurse who had known her father, who had sat by Sissy's side the night when she woke after her operation in utter terror.

Her time in the hospital was still on Sissy's mind in the late afternoon. After her mother went out, Sissy let herself into her father's study. It was a small room, north-west facing, sunny in the afternoons, but today there was no sun. The cloud resting low on the hills was not dense or heavy but light, so loosely held together that Sissy could almost see the vapour from which it was formed. At times, the cloud poured down towards the water, seeming to disappear into the surface of the harbour as if it were being stroked gently from above.

Sissy knelt on the carpet, feeling cold from the cellar cavity seep up between the floorboards. She pulled an encyclopaedia from the bottom shelf and opened it out on the floor. Old white in its centre with creamy-brown edges where the light had touched it, the paper was not yet foxed. *On the eve of her wedding,* she read, *after trying on her white woollen bridal tunic and veil the colour of flame, the Roman bride-to-be (usually aged between 12 and 14) would dedicate her bulla to the goddess of the crossroads. As well as presiding over the place where three roads met, Trivia was also Queen of Ghosts, goddess of witchcraft, sorcery and graveyards, who wandered at night and was known by the barking of dogs.*

Sissy sat back on her haunches. She had always thought of crossroads as cross-shaped, the meeting place of four roads. It was suddenly clear to her that the Roman idea was entirely different—no straight ahead, no simple left or right. According to her father's old dictionary of etymology, *trivia* had also come to mean a common place or gutter. It seemed strange that the word's meaning had changed from the name of a goddess worthy of the gratitude of every girl who made it safely through the perilous years of childhood to a word used to describe things of small value, of little importance, insignificant things.

When Amanda returned, they sat at the table in the front room, looking out at the late light on the low tide water of the harbour, eating a meal of salmon, new potatoes and salad.

Amanda said, as if resuming an unfinished conversation, 'And I remember how annoyed I was.'

'Annoyed about what?'

'That time when you were in hospital. It was the first time that I had been away after your father died. We'd all just sat down to dinner and I got the phone call to say that you were in hospital. So I thought, well, there's nothing I can do about it. I may as well eat.'

'But you've always said that you left the conference straight away. That you missed out on the banquet.'

'That did happen. But I couldn't have driven all that way back without eating. And I had a few extra drinks as well. I knew that if they'd breathalysed me, I would have had the perfect excuse.'

'Oh.'

'The nurses kept asking me why I didn't come and see you very often. I'd already told them that I had a business to run. They didn't like me pointing out that that's what *they're* paid to do. When they sent you home, I had to stay in this house for six whole weeks.'

Sissy put down her knife and fork and drained the wine in her glass to the very last drop. Then, picking up the bottle, she refilled her mother's glass and her own. The place where they were sitting, almost exactly where she was seated at that moment, was the same place where, all those years ago, her father had lain for his last weeks. Her mother carried on eating, and the conversation changed direction, and though Sissy joined in, taking sip after sip of wine, refilling their glasses once more and then once more again, her mind was still far back in time.

Not long after Sissy returned to school after recovering from her operation, her puberty began and the charmed unawareness of her childhood loosened and was lost. In its place came the fluorescence of adolescence, bathing everything in its harsh, too bright light. All that was absent could never again go unnoticed, as on the night in the hospital when she woke alone and felt the blood beneath her, and of all of the other nights when she waited in the darkness of the evening for her mother to return to the place that Sissy had been told, since her earliest years, was her home.

* Impressionism *

LAST NIGHT I DREAMT that I stole blueberries from your freezer, lifted them from the mist and frost as if from a sarcophagus of ice. I must explain that I have never stolen anything in my life, but, in my dream, I had conned my way into your house by offering to do your cleaning. Whilst inside, I filched the blueberries and wrapped them in my teal blue dressing gown, which lay, with dream logic, nearby. Though the blueberries were frozen, somehow, I'd left evidence, a trail of dull, purple handprints, and I used the cord of my gown to wipe all traces away.

In the kitchen, while your back was turned, I took some loose change from the jar of coins on your counter before smiling, saying goodbye to you, and hurrying home. As for you, you looked at me with utter suspicion, no witness to my crimes and yet aware that I was guilty.

I think of you infrequently, perhaps once or twice a year, but lately I've been preoccupied by might-have-beens. We had the necessary qualifications for friendship—similar interests, mutual friends—yet friends we never were. It's rather like getting an ear worm, not being able to stop singing an irritating tune: however much you hate it, it's stuck in your brain, driving you mad. And it's not as if anything actually happened, so why is it bothering me?

All this began a few weeks ago, when your name started cycling through my head one Friday night. I was up late and alone on the sofa (in the same teal blue dressing gown, thinking I should get up and go to bed, because I don't usually sit on the sofa alone late at night, but I couldn't seem to start moving). After your name appeared, I thought of the fairy cakes, dry in my throat, and the children, who are so much bigger now, as they were then, pressing shapes into play dough, on that day so long ago when my voice got stuck.

How had it happened? The dryness, the stuck words, after the fluency of our first meeting, that silky, exciting conversation that flowed like water over smooth, smooth pebbles, that ranged from Antarctica to Iceland, from Dunedin street names to that thin place, Iona, from mermaids to bathtubs, all of it lost, dissolved, crumbs in my throat I couldn't swallow then, crumbs I still can't swallow.

In our old house, near the end of the corridor which led from the front door to the kitchen, was a dining room. The room was dark and yet I always liked it. Its low sash window looked out into a courtyard filled with pots of plants which tolerate low light—a *Fatsia japonica*, ferns, a *Viburnum tinus*.

We sat in this room the day you came to visit. I had made fairy cakes, and the children helped me to ice them. I got the nicer cups out, the ones without chips on their rims. I was thinking, I suppose, of the way we used to do things in Dunedin when we'd go round to visit friends. There was always tea made in a pot and vintage plates and cups before they were fashionable. We used them because we were poor, living in flats, and most things we owned and used—crockery, cutlery, clothes, furniture—was second hand; strange that everyone wants it now, this old stuff, the patterned plates and cups. There were always cakes, made or bought, to show you'd made an effort, to show your visitor you cared. And, in fact, the darkness of the room was also like the darkness inside some of those old Dunedin houses, so perhaps I was trying to recreate something without realising it, to scroll backwards fifteen years to an earlier time in my life.

So, as you could have seen, had you noticed, I had been looking forward to seeing you, had made an effort with the cups and cakes, and I'd tidied, but you didn't seem to notice anything; you seemed uncomfortable, said little. You knew I had children but still, they seemed to surprise you. Or perhaps it was the house, a little, shabby, ordinary terrace house, the walls of the dining room covered in glittery children's handprints, drawings, paintings.

That table was where so much happened: every meal and every making session, paying bills and working out budgets. Earlier in the day, I'd filled old ice cream tubs with sand and spread play dough on trays and the children had made shapes in them, pressing down anything they could find, and then filling the spaces with feathers, with torn up pieces of paper. As I sat there with you, I was tired for the usual reasons; another broken night, another early start, a busy morning, breakfast, snacks and lunch, frantic tidying up and making the blasted cakes.

You'd wanted to come at three in the afternoon, a bit of a dead time, the older child flagging but no longer taking a nap, the younger one unable to settle because of the unusual activity—three in the afternoon was the time of fair-weather walks, of rocking-to-sleeps, of desperate afternoon videos. A cup of tea and a cake and a little, listless chat—no mermaids this time, no gold pouring onto a Hebridean beach from a nearly accessible heaven—and me feeling for the first time all that

I wasn't, hollow, transparent as a pillar of light, but not in a good way (not with the pure emptiness of a saint or the rewarded deprivation of an ascetic) but because I was seeing myself as you saw me. Then, after crumbling some cake in your fingers, after half an hour perhaps, you went and after that I did not hear from you for such a long time.

So long ago but, when I think of it, I can feel my younger child's small body pressed against mine, see my older child's dazzling smile and sparkling eyes and hear her bright talk—the smell of them, the weight and touch of them, which all these years on I still feel in my left hip as an ache.

The first time we met was at a reading group. It took place in a café, an upstairs room, one of the oldest buildings in town, Jacobean, maybe, which would have been here when Byron walked these streets. We talked about Iceland and holy wells, old tin baths set before the fire, the darkness inside those Dunedin villas, an orange-enamelled teapot filled with red-pink camellias we both remembered on the kitchen table of one of those houses, and I said to myself, *I've made a new friend*.

But now I think about it, I'd seen you even before that, reading an excerpt from your novel and seven (or is it eight?) years later it's just been published. And I wouldn't have known, but I was sitting on the sofa late at night and your name started running through my head, repeating and repeating, though I hardly ever think of you, and so I went to the computer and looked you up and there it was, the news that your book had been released that very day.

And I started to think again about what had happened between us, which was nothing of course, and why I had ended up feeling hurt by it and slighted. I still feel uneasy thinking of us sitting around that table, the cake sticking in my throat, the words drying in my mouth. And of sitting in another dark room where my computer was, sending emails that you didn't often respond to, or, if you did, only after days, weeks even, had passed.

At times I wonder what my life might have been like with different echoes coming back rather than the sound of my footsteps passing outwards, unimpeded, towards some far edge, and I remember how you spoke of what you called the perfect quiet; it occurred sometimes during a performance, a quality of listening that could tell you whether you were on the right track. That's what I'm doing here, writing into the silence, waiting to hear what doesn't come back.

Another friend came into my life, someone with whom I did not have much in common except that we both had children, and after that I was ill with an infection that took months to shift. I remember it as one of my lowest times. Then came another disaster which submerged my life for four whole years. I stopped caring about anything unnecessary.

The last time I saw you, a friend invited me to one of your events. You'd moved on by then, were living overseas. You read some new work and I listened to you, and I listened to the audience listening to you; I listened to see if I could hear that quality you'd described. I couldn't, and I wondered whether what you were trying to write would one day become good, or whether, like so many other things that had barely had a chance to happen, your heart had already gone out of it.

* Shepherd's Bush Blues *

AFTER FINDING THE RIGHT house number, she knocked on the door. She had spoken to Michael about the room, pushing ten-pence pieces into the slot of the payphone every minute or so. When the door opened, he stood before her, stooping against his tallness, his salmon-pink shirt crumpled, its top button missing, the collar held almost closed by a keyboard tie, a faint sheen of sweat glittering on his forehead. He wiped his palms down the front of his jeans before shaking her hand and then beckoned her upstairs into the kitchen; its floor was covered in cork tiles, its walls painted warm red, the cupboard doors deep blue.

As Michael asked her questions she tried to read, upside down, what was written on the piece of paper which lay on the table in front of him. *6pm, Lottie, 29, Neurologist. 6.15, Zeno, 25, Musician. 6.30, Rasa, 33, Chiropodist.* And so on. A list of a dozen names at least. Her name at the bottom of the list. *9.30pm. 22. From New Zealand. In London for a year. Travelling.* Will he choose me, she wondered, or a neurologist? What are the chances?

'Mind if I smoke?' She reached into the plastic bag, made of sturdy, shiny forest green plastic, which served as her handbag, her hand tightening around her lighter and her packet of B&H.

'Not at all,' Michael said.

'Want one?'

'Yes, please. I don't usually. I have to limit my vices. Can't afford both fags and booze. Booze won. The flat isn't even worth what I paid for it. I have to get some more money in, or I'll end up on the streets.'

He showed her the bedroom which had been his, the room that now, to cover costs, he was forced to let out. Beyond the window she glimpsed a narrow garden, a fence, the backs and roofs of other houses which glittered under the streetlights, a dark sea stretching towards Acton, Ealing Broadway, the runways of Heathrow. At home, the houses had all been different shapes and sizes, their iron roofs brightly painted, and green-black hills dotted with gorse, a harbour filled, at low tide, with dun-coloured sandbanks and, out at the heads, the wild green sea: she had never been surrounded by so much sameness, such uniformity of shape, such monotony of colour. From somewhere nearby came a faint repetitive sound, as if a gate or door were banging in the wind.

'It seems so safe,' she said, turning away from the window. 'It feels as if nothing bad could happen here.' But Michael was not behind her. He had stepped out of the room when her back was turned. She looked around at the futon, the chest of drawers. On the wall was an exhibition poster, a water colour painting of Indian horsemen, perhaps an old book illustration. The horsemen were looking at something in the distance, beyond the picture's edge, wearing expressions of surprise and something close to wonder, as they rode amongst plants whose branches, thick and cactus-like, were raised towards the sky like handless arms.

'It's lovely,' she said, when Michael came back. 'What a lovely room.'

'It's yours.' His eyes looked red, as if they were enflamed. 'If you want it. If you're sure you can pay.'

'I can pay. I've got a job.'

There was also a box room, Michael's office, and the front room, where he now slept. They would share the bathroom, which was through a doorway and two steps down from the kitchen. On the way to the tube station, it occurred to her that she had nothing to bring to it but her backpack which, for two or three weeks, had been propped against the wall of a friend's bedsit in Camden and the green plastic bag containing her wallet and cigarettes and keys.

On the night after she moved in, grubby from work, wanting to scrub the gritty layer of city grime off her, she ran a deeper bath than usual. She was used to showers but there was no shower here and as she slipped into the water, the heat and immersion made her giddy for a moment. She closed her eyes and the steam rose up around her as she slid back until the water coated her shoulders. Her eyes were still closed when the noises began; dull, heavy sounds that came from the beneath the floor, as if furniture were being shifted from one place to another.

Were the downstairs neighbours moving something? A refrigerator? A dishwasher? It seemed an odd time of night to be shifting furniture. Thud, thud. Pause. Thud. And voices, muffled. A man's voice, shouting incomprehensibly. All at once the bath water seemed both too hot and too cold, and the skin on her face prickled with heat. She pulled the plug and then climbed out as noisily as possible, feeling the tug of the water against her calves as it sidled down the plughole and away.

She got back into her clothes and hurried downstairs. No lights were on in the flat below. She could hear nothing; no shouting, no sounds of shifting, only the dim oceanic noise of traffic passing on the Uxbridge Road. Walking as far as the nearest Londis, she bought a great bunch of daffodils, shoutingly yellow, because, since arriving in London, they were the first bright thing she had seen; the man behind the counter, perhaps bewildered by her enthusiasm, or perhaps because the flowers were past their best, sold them to her cheaply.

By the time she got back to the corner of her road, the lights of The Princess Caroline were switched off, but the chip shop was still open. The Greek owner stood in the doorway, handing a steaming bundle to a man in a torn coat. Under one of the picnic tables outside the pub, a tangle of plastic and the inside of a sleeping bag gleamed white on the stained ground.

In the kitchen, Michael sat the table, his head propped on his hand, a row of Tennent's Super cans marching away from his elbow. In front of him were a line of little animals, made from folded paper.

'Where have you been?' Michael said.

'I decided to go out. For a walk.'

'At this time of night?'

'I brought some daffodils. For you.' As she shoved them towards him, she saw his eyes fill with tears.

'Thank you,' he said. 'You shouldn't have.'

She had not meant to give them to him, but when she had seen his face she had had to. Michael had once worked in a gallery owned by an Indian prince, the sound of whose name made her think of heaped piles of glittering treasure, but all that remained of that time was the poster of the horsemen, dark red and dirt blue, riding into the desert, the negative equity, the views of the road and of the sea of roofs. Now Michael worked with a theatre company, folding animals from paper for an audience of children.

'How was the performance?'

'It was fine. Fine. The elephant collapsed at one

point, but the children thought it was part of the act. They laughed their heads off.'

'What time did you finish?'

'Six. I went out with the actors afterwards.' Michael ground his palms into his forehead. 'I shouldn't have.'

'It sounds like fun.'

'Fun? No, it's not fun. You've no idea what they're like.' Michael banged the table as he spoke, knocking the little paper creatures sideways. 'The actors are the worst. They drink more than anyone I have ever known but it seems to do them no harm. If anything, the opposite seems to be true; it seems to give them strength whereas, with me, it only makes things worse.'

As if he were not already weak enough, the silence that followed his outburst seemed to say. And then she heard the noise, the scraping, shifting sound, coming from downstairs.

'They can't still be moving stuff. Not at this time of night,' she said.

'What are you talking about?'

'The people downstairs. Have they just moved in?'

'No. They've been there for years. What did you hear?'

'When I was in the bath, I heard...I heard...That sound. There. Like they're moving things.'

'It's him. He hits her.' Michael yanked off one of his Chelsea boots and dropped to the floor, whacking the sole ferociously against the boards. 'Stop it, you bastard,' he screamed. 'Or I'll call the police again. Stop it now, do you hear?'

In bed, in her lovely room, she listened to the silence. The aftertaste of the cheap white wine she'd been drinking at the table with Michael, mixed with toothpaste, lingered nastily in her mouth.

With her next wage packet, she bought herself a new handbag. Thinking that the green plastic bag might come in useful sometime in the future, she laid it in the bottom drawer before placing the flaccid carcass of her backpack on top of it. Her scant possessions barely filled one of the higher drawers. Though she had lowered herself into the bath with some trepidation each night, there had been no repetition of the noises from downstairs.

One day she woke up and it was spring. As the birds came back and took possession of the hedges, the man who had been sleeping under the picnic table moved on. For some time, scraps of his carrier bags remained lodged in the spokes of the privet hedge beside the pub. A few decent rain showers washed away the stains and the smell so that anyone who had not seen him would never know that he had been there at all. The Greek man from the chip shop still stood in his doorway, gazing up and down the Uxbridge Road, never looking, it seemed, for anyone in particular. When she passed, he called out to her, 'What are you having?' Sometimes he called her darling, as if she were just that, his jewel amongst the fryers and the bricks.

One evening, she found Michael at the kitchen table, folding the phone bill into the shape of a frog. Pressing the back of the paper with his finger, he made it leap across the table towards her. From two yellow parking tickets, he folded a peacock with a fanned tail.

'My friend from Camden is coming for dinner. Want to eat with us, Michael?'

'That would be great. I'll go to the offy and get some wine.'

She had been spending more time with her friend from Camden. Sometimes he worked at a clinic around the corner from her. If she was not working, they had lunch together.

One empty bottle of Romanian red wine stood on the floor by the refrigerator, another stood open on the table. Michael topped up their glasses, the wine matching almost exactly the other red tones of the kitchen.

'What are those blobs on the roof over there?' The friend from Camden asked.

'Cat turds,' said Michael. 'There are too many cats and not enough territory to go around so the cats have to crap on the roofs.'

That night, after her friend from Camden had left, lying in bed, the noises began again. Scrape, thud. Thud, thud. If the noise continued, she would have to go into the front room and wake Michael. He knew the names of the couple downstairs, as the police knew his, because he had reported these incidents to them so many times before. Pushing back the covers, she placed her feet on the cold floor. *I cannot stand this for much longer.* By the time she reached the door, the noises had stopped, but still she thought, *I cannot live with this. I cannot live here anymore.*

The next day, she waited for Michael to come home with her weekly rent money—two twenty-pound notes, one ten and one five—in a pile on the table in front of her. When Michael returned, he might fold them into snails or frogs, birds or deer; he might turn them into something they were not. He was the only person she knew who had the power to bring them briefly to life.

By the time she and the friend from Camden had found a house to share in the countryside outside the city, it was summer. She had not been able to look Michael in the eye when she gave in her notice. He began interviewing flatmates again, dressed in his crumpled salmon-pink shirt and keyboard tie. When she came to pack up her possessions, she found that she had acquired, in a few months, many more than would now fit into her backpack.

On her last day, waking, as she looked around the bedroom at the futon, the empty pin-board, the poster of the horsemen, eager-eyed, in pursuit of something in the distance only they could see—something more, surely, than those cactus-like trees—she remembered that she had woken in the middle of the night and thought she had heard someone calling her name.

When she went into the kitchen, Michael was not there. He had left no note for her on the table, no row of folded animals. All she had left to do was to take her bag and let herself out before posting the keys back through the letterbox. But as she was walking down the stairs, she had the overwhelming feeling that she had forgotten something of such vital importance that her life could not properly continue unless she found it.

Going back into the room that had, for a brief time, been hers, she lifted the mattress and checked underneath it before slowly opening the drawers, one by one. In the lowest drawer was the green plastic bag she had used as a handbag on the first night she had come here, a thing so familiar, so negligible, that she had almost lost her ability to see it, as if it were that easy to shrug off what she had seen and heard and felt, to leave what she had so recently been behind her.

* Peregian *

ON THIS PART OF the coast, the scrub-covered dunes remain unbuilt-up, close to natural. Not like Surfer's, with its skyscrapers and apartment blocks, taverns and bottle stores, arcades full of pokey machines and malls full of shops. Here no loudspeakers blast music onto the beach. No towering buildings cast shadows on the sand in the afternoon.

After the fiercest heat of the day has passed, they walk from the holiday house down a quiet residential street to a pathway in the band of bush, lined with tea-trees, spindly gums and spiky-leaved shrubs. Although it is after three, the sand still burns and the waves are strong and green.

Kelly and Ashley race into the sea, tee-shirts over their togs to stop the tops of their shoulders burning. Even though she's seventeen, the boiling thuds knock Kelly sideways. Sand scours her face, the inside of her ears. Tiny grains are wedged between her teeth. She glances at her cousin, barely ten and skinny, to see if he's okay, then gestures to him to head landwards. The light on the water's surface dazzles her eyes; the line of skin on her scalp where her hair is parted is painfully hot. As she dunks her head under to soothe it, water rushes up her nose. Surfacing, she hears her aunt and uncle calling them back to the shore.

The sea tries to rake her back, but she slips its grip and lumps over to her towel. Ashley staggers out of the waves, reeling a little. After dropping to his knees, he slams his hands into a ring of sandcastles. Maddie, her little cousin, fills flower-shaped moulds and tips them out, making the sand seem embossed, tactile as Anaglypta.

As the warm breeze dries her, Kelly slaps more suncream on her pale skin. Her aunt passes out cartons from an Eski bin.

'Chocolate or strawberry? Drink it before it gets too warm.'

The cool milk tastes thin compared to the rich, creamy stuff she's used to. Kelly wiggles her toes. The tops of her feet are nicely sand scoured, their rough edges smoothed. She bends her knee back to examine her sole, rubbing her thumb over the dry edges of her heel. It's so hot here, day and night, she doesn't wear shoes. It's a joy to walk barefoot on the floorboards, but the soles of her feet have turned an inky sepia brown, as if the oil which darkens the hardwood has seeped into her skin. The action of the waves has lightened but not eliminated the stain.

Yesterday, Ashley said to her, 'Your feet are filthy. Just looking at them makes me want to puke.'

'He's going to be a hygiene inspector when he grows up,' her aunt had said. 'So pernickety. He gets that from his German grandmother. She used to starch all of his father's clothes. Even his undies.'

Ashley, blushing, had spread his hands over his cheeks. His mother likes to tease him, her lilting voice nasal and sharpish, though she always smiles as if to undercut each verbal jab. Her uncle doesn't speak much. When he does, his voice is gentle. Though large, he is still and quiet, able to blend into his surroundings as he is doing now, flat on his back on the sand, a gently rippling newspaper laid over his face.

Her cousins are golden skinned with dark blond hair. Her aunt has a beautiful face, narrow and long, its features symmetrical. Her uncle is beer-bellied, and the hair that was once on his head appears to have migrated south to his back and stomach. Maddie, bored with making sand-flowers, climbs his chest and pulls hairs from it until he squeals.

The wind carries the smell of far islands out in the Pacific, of ripening fruit and sweet and cloying flowers which open in the morning and fall that very night, the scent of them so strong she almost expects to see the waves deposit a load of blooms alongside the shells and the occasional piece of shiny, hard weed.

This evening, as she has done every other evening, her aunt will walk around the verandah which rings the stilted house, picking flowers from the plants that scramble up its sides. She, her aunt and Maddie, fresh from their post-beach showers, will choose one to tuck behind their ears, easing it into their still wet, newly washed hair. She will help her aunt place clean vine leaves on the platters, ready to be loaded with food for the dinner table; she will float the remaining hibiscus and frangipani blossoms on the surface of curved glass vases full of water.

'I'm bored,' Ashley says.

'How can you be bored' her aunt asks, 'when you have all this?'

'I can't sit here any longer. I want to go for a walk. Dad?'

'He's asleep.'

'Not again. Mum?'

'I can't leave Maddie. Kelly will take you, won't you, Kelly?'

'Okay.'

'For God's sake, Ashley, leave your jandals here. You're only going to be walking on sand.'

They set out, following the curve of wave wash. The sun, behind them, still burning hot, is slipping downwards, off the tender parts of her scalp and shoulders to her back. When they turn and wave again, the sun's so low and bright they have to shield their eyes and, even then, she is not sure she can see her aunt and uncle and Maddie, the little nest of towels and stuff they've left behind.

'Do you want to go any further?'

'Yes,' says Ashley. 'Let's keep going.'

Ashley, who is in his last year of primary, asks her about high school. *What are exams like? What's your school like?*

'Have you got a boyfriend?' Ashley says.

'With feet this dirty, who'd want me?'

He puts his hands over his cheeks.

'Ashley, I'm joking.'

'Mum says I've got no sense of humour.'

'I'm sure you have. That's *her* thing, isn't it? If you both told jokes, it might spoil it for your mum. Divide the audience. Don't worry about it.'

Next time they turn the sun is balanced on the edge of some inland range and the sky around it is orange, pink and, in its further reaches, green.

Ashley says, 'Maybe we should go back now.'

'It's dark so quickly here. I'd forgotten.' Her hometown lies two thousand miles to the south; further from the equator, twilight is prolonged. How long have they been walking for? She'd taken her watch off to go swimming, left it with her bag back on her towel.

They turn and begin to walk back, the still warm sand cooling beneath their feet. Around them, a sudden and convincing darkness settles. The incoming tide pushes them landwards, higher and higher up the beach. The less firm sand is harder going, and needle-sharp, spiky bits from the bank of bush are buried in it.

Ashley says, 'We should go up that way, towards those lights. This must be the way.'

She tries to picture the place they are staying in, sees a villa-lined curving road, tin roofs wet with light. They scramble through bushes, following what looks like a path but isn't. As they scale a fence, spiders' webs and other sheer, sticky things brush their faces. The night around them loud with insect ticks and clicks and the lower tump of frogs. Finally, a residential road. What colour was their holiday house? Was it smoky blue-grey like that place over there? She had not been paying attention, does not know the name of the road or the house's number. But Ashley knows.

'Peregian,' Ashley is saying. 'Is this Peregian?'

'I don't know.' As they pass the houses, security lights snap on, but their interiors are dark. When they reach the highway there are no shops: no pizza restaurant, no dairy and no surf club.

Which way should they walk? Ashley wants to turn left.

'Right' she says. 'Let's try right.' As they step onto the road, the warm edge of the asphalt oozes; a fringe of tar sticks to their feet, collecting a bristle of small stones and hard pieces of leaf. They try to walk side by side but are blinded by the light and noise and speed of cars flashing past them. Ashley's toes, stubbed on the road surface, begin to bleed.

He is crying now, perhaps in pain or fear or because he is angry that his feet are dirty. She cannot guess and it doesn't seem a good time to ask. To protect him from the cars, she tries standing on the outside of him with her arm around his shoulder, but it forces him further into the barbed leaf litter. He trails behind her for a while, and she finds herself turning every few moments to check on him. When they come to a bend, they decide to cross over so that the cars will be coming from behind them, and their lights will not be so blinding. On the other side, she pulls him in front of her and puts her hand on his shoulder.

She is not sure how it has come to this. A short time ago they were walking on the beach and everything was all right. All they had to do was to turn around and it was all there waiting for them: the towels, the sand flowers, the warming chocolate milk, her uncle and aunt and her little cousin. Behind them, the traffic doesn't slow down so much as brake, speeding past them too fast to do anything else, the car taillights bright as flame.

They're walking uphill now. She doesn't remember there being any hills on the drive down. She didn't take notice of anything that might help them now. Keep going, that's the only thing to do, and hope they come to some sort of settlement, or shop, or service station or…

'Ashley.'

'What?'

'Do you want to stop for a bit?'

'This is all your fault.'

'What do you mean?'

'If you hadn't come to stay with us, none of this would've happened.'

'I don't understand.'

'You're ugly and you're dirty, not just your feet, and your clothes are awful. All worn out like rags, that's what Mum said. That's why she took you shopping and…'

'Ashley, stop. I know you're upset but…'

'You shut up. You just shut up. And stop looking at me with your ugly face. I hate you, and I want you to go away. I don't want you to stay with us.'

He speeds up as if trying to race away from her, moving right onto the road margin, while cars beep and swerve to avoid him.

'Ashley. Come on, this is no place to run. Ashley, stop it. Come back now.'

On the other side of the road, a car sounds its horn but does not stop.

This time the car approaching behind them is already driving slowly, yellow hazards flashing, the stones and leaves cracking beneath its wheels as it pulls up on the painful verge. When they reach it, the windows are already rolled down, the passenger doors pushed open.

Her uncle, in his quiet voice, is telling Ashley to stop crying, not to make a fuss over something as unimportant thing as the state of his feet. It's only a matter of time before the tar washes off, and the wounds on his toes heal. Her uncle is saying that he never doubted that she'd keep him safe until they were found, despite the unknown territory.

As they close the doors and her uncle pulls away, all she can think is that she's missed the part of the evening she likes the best. The nights they sit around the table won't be the same. Tonight, when they get back, her aunt won't be holding out a tray of flowers, smiling at her as she chooses one to slip into her hair. When the blooms are large, sometimes the petals brush against her cheek; it's as if she can feel that cool touch now, against her dry, sand-coated skin, but when she lifts her hand there's nothing there.

* Par Temps de Pluie *

I SQUEEZE MY WAY through the crowded lobby and down a passageway lined with marble sculptures to a bright white atrium and a curving marble stair. At the entrance to the gallery, I show my ticket for the exhibition and the guard waves me through. Upstairs, on the white walls, hang paintings of clouds, sprayed chalk on slate, simple and ethereal, traces of the scantest precipitation created by a desert-dwelling artist homesick for English gloom.

In the next room, rooks on branches, a tumble of stark black-whiteness, dead stalks of sunflowers carrying heads of rotting seed. And in front of a giant painting of an avalanche, you, you, you: the closed door of the past I am not ready to knock on, to open and step through.

A frozen moment. From the first time we met there was something between us. I wouldn't call it love, exactly—it was more like recognition. I open my mouth to say your name but then, no, no. I turn. I do not know where to begin. I do not know what to say.

The room, so quiet when I came in, is fuller now, the slide and slap of people in the high white space, the blurry wave-sound of traffic in the darkening lane below. A feeling then, a burning ear, a prickle of attention, the old instinct which tells us we are known, are seen. Though my back is turned, I know you're looking, know that soon the snow will slide off the mountainside like a wall. How cold that weight, the huge crush, the white silence. I hear it groan and loosen and I run.

Outside, in Piccadilly, I lose myself in crowds. It's fully

dark now. I walk these streets as I have always walked them, in summer's warmth and winter's dark. This place was once low forest, birch and hazel, marginal land near the edge of the Thames. Despite the hardness of the grey paving, I feel it still beneath my fur-lined boots; earth springy with moss and damp, softened by the river's thousand fingers creeping outward through the soil. Millennia ago, people came here from every corner of the country to worship the river's dark water. They carried with them the smoothest, whitest, roundest stones they could find, offered them to her current with their praise and prayers. Here, once, little birds sang loud in the sedge, clung tightly to the swaying reeds, their tiny, dun bodies hidden in the flicker of golden-green sunlight sieved through leaves.

Long gone the marsh, but a scent of it's still here, beneath these wet, grey slabs. I turn into Green Park, stripped of its flowers by order of a long-ago queen. You never gave me flowers. Only a sign, once. A white envelope with my name scrawled on it; inside, a single blade of fresh, green grass.

It's so hard to see things as they are. That's why, although I always loved it and love it still, I moved away from here. My gaze was downcast, my hearing and my seeing, all my senses dimmed. Too much blue-grey hard stone, too much traffic, the constant jostle of bodies. I needed earth and trees, the scent of rain on granite, cloud shadows tearing like wild horses across fields and red-brown cliffs. I settled by the rock-dark, boiling ocean, under the reaches of a star-struck sky. Such things I've seen since I've been there. Yesterday, out at sea, a line of lemon-green was resting on the waves, and through the wet, a washed-out rainbow stretched between two headlands like a net.

Light snow is falling. I retrace my steps through the park, from whose fine beds a foolish king picked flowers for his mistress. In the church where Blake worshipped as a child, I slide into a pew. The flowers near the altar—guelder rose and amaryllis, poppy heads and amaranthus—speak to me of what could have been.

That last night on Long Acre we ate a meal of oysters, scallops, lobster, sitting on high stools at a marble-topped table. We drank tall flutes of gold-grey champagne, tipped back our heads to swallow the pearls of scented bubbles melting in our mouths. You asked if I could taste the flavours hidden within the wine—hints of dark cherry and vanilla, blood orange and saffron—and I thought for a moment I could sense them on my tongue, as strange and haunting as a half-remembered song. The air hung heavy from days of tired heat, from burning hours of sun; from the mouth of the underground rose a fetid, fumy, swampy, dirty dampness. But always, with you, that sense of implacable cold, rising from the table's marble surface to fill the empty oyster shells and the cracked lobster husks, spent crescents of lemons, heaps of crushed ice melting on silver platters.

On the way home it rained, warm and sweet. We sheltered under the trees in the park, the place stripped of its every petal by a queen's fury. When a flock of gulls wheeled and screamed above us, you said it meant there was a storm at sea. I looked up and watched the soaring wings. There, caught in the streetlight, the kite of a raptor flew over the rooftops of the Ritz.

That night I couldn't sleep. I watched the rain thicken and boil and turn to storm. Dreamless, I listened to the rain's long song. Even after the oysters and the promises, I was fading, a spark off a flint thrown far from its kindling, a ghost at my own feast.

In the morning, when you'd left for work, I packed my things and ran from your perch amongst leaded roofs, attic dormers and copper domes, past towers whose mercury facades glimmered and faded in the steam. In the flowerless park, I stopped to draw in breath. Nearby, snow geese and swans circled in water made dun green by effluent and weed. I hunched to ease the tightening in my chest. The choice was clear: to run, or to spend my life here, crouched beneath high, unstable peaks. That night, I caught a train west, the sleeper to the sea.

Footsteps on the path behind me, echoing in the winter dark, wanting to turn but not wanting to, not wanting to know, to see, to hear. The heartbreak and the blame.

You in the park, on the green-painted bench, a sparrow eating crumbs from your fingers. You in the restaurant, holding the white-grey oyster shell, tipping it up to your lips. A series of flashes: marble-topped tables, silver platters, lobsters in their coral armour, lemon juice shivering on oyster flesh. The iodine tang of ocean, high, bronze cliffs, a wide, white, empty beach, the surf-song of the waves, the bluebell mirrors of the Porthmeor tide pools, the dazzle and the glitter of the sand.

A charcoal sky empty but for a cloud so light and wispy it is barely there, a handful of vapour caught above the dry, hot earth, which holds within it every dream of home.

Breathe. Breathe. Breathe. One lasting, deeper breath, and only then turn. Only then turn into the cold.

So much rain on centuries of snow. Decades of snow, layer upon layer, built up until it falls—falls so that every light goes out, the village gone along with its people, the whitest whiteness that encloses, smothers, covers, and all that was beneath it whitely lost.

∗ Girls on Motorbikes ∗

RAINEY HEARS THE MOTORBIKE before she sees it. It's making a put-put sound, as if backfiring, as if oil or the white dust of the road is clogging the engine up, stopping the sparks from shooting effortlessly across the plugs. As the bike bumps over the ridge of unsealed road and into the driveway, she sees blond hair poking out from beneath the rider's helmet. The woman, who could be any age, carries a round, black ball on her lap. When she steps off the bike, kicks out the stand and hangs it from the handlebars next to her own, Rainey sees it's a second helmet.

Out in the carport, a familiar scythe-shaped face beneath blond synthetic tresses.

'Edie?'

'It's a wig.' Edie tugs at the long, blond locks.

Underneath, Edie's hair is black and straight, cut into a shiny bob. Side on, she's all sharp lines, as if she's stepped straight off an Egyptian carving.

'What do you think?'

It makes her look like Andy Warhol. There's a good chance Edie doesn't know who Andy Warhol is. 'I like it. It looks great.'

'What are you doing?'

'Nothing.'

'Come for a ride.'

'You haven't got a licence.'

'I pinched my sister's.'

'Where do you want to go?'

'I dunno. Anywhere.'

'Okay.'

On the back of the bike, hands clasped round Edie's waist, Rainey wishes she'd changed out of her shorts and put jeans on. Edie wears night blue overalls, the type worn by mechanics. Only Edie could make them seem desirable, like some recent, unattainably expensive fashion.

On the unsealed road, the white dust flies around them until, with a bump, they join the tarmac's black. The air is full of the smell of pine and herbs. The lake is blue and flat. Outside the shops, Edie pulls up and they step off the bike.

Edie asks, 'Have you got money?' When she takes her helmet off the wig comes too and she passes it to Rainey. 'You put it on.'

'No, thanks.'

'Go on.'

The net and ribs dig into Rainey's scalp. Artificial hair on top of her own wild mass and the sun's blade striking down on both.

'Oh, my God, your hair, Rainey. Your hair is an utter shambles.' After snatching it back, Edie tucks the wig into the front of her overalls.

Without the wig, Edie seems less strange, less stunning, because her looks are once again familiar. Edie's beauty, at fourteen, causes boys anguish. Grown men, too. They don't know what to make of her, the kind of girl who wears a blond, synthetic wig and orange-rimmed sunglasses, the kind of girl who rides a motorbike in overalls.

Someone once plaited Edie's hair in braids tipped by coloured beads so she looked even more like Nefertiti. Edie's life will always be extraordinary. Behind her she'll trail this sense of imminent apocalypse, not for herself but for those who dare to follow in her wake.

They rattle along the tree-lined lakeshore road through deep drifts of gravel, bouncing from pools of shade to pools of light. The lake, calm and flat, seems solid, as if it could be made of hard, blue ice. Rainey wants to tell Edie to steer out on it and then they'll speed across its reaches to the dark, bush-covered haunches of the mountains. They'll stop off at the islands, first Mou Wahu, jolt up the track to reach the tarn whose waters fall and rise as if with breath. In the burnt-out ruins of the old hotel on Emerald Island, they'll lie beneath yellow-leaved willows self-seeded in the silver gravel. They'll kick off their jandals and paddle, their feet minnow-pale in the greenish shallows of the vast, black-hearted lake.

At the pine tree-covered point, the bike splutters out.

'Shit.' Edie kicks a tyre. 'We're out of petrol.'

As Rainey dismounts, her bare calf touches burning hot exhaust pipe and she flinches. Edie sits down at a concrete picnic table. Deep shade from the trees all around. Beneath their feet is a carpet of pine needles, sharp smelling as Dettol. Amber sap oozes from the stems of dislodged pinecones.

At school, in biology lessons, Rainey has been studying the life cycle of pine trees. Gymnosperm is the correct botanical term. When the time is right, pollen from the male cone floats onto a female cone, fertilising it. The seeds produced are naked, not held within a fruit's protective flesh. Once the seeds develop, the cone's hard scales open like the petals of a flower, become brittle, fall.

The cones on the ground have tightly closed scales, a

rigid armour. They look stricken, as if shaken from their destiny by some freakish, passing storm. But in the whole time Rainey has been at the lake, three weeks or more, there has been no bad weather, just hot, blue days like this one, one after another after another.

Rainey and Edie have been to bonfire parties on this point at which teenagers like them sit drinking warm beer. Boys drag driftwood washed up on the lakeshore into a rough circle and pour lighter fluid on it. They sit with their faces towards the flames, the cold hand of the alpine night pressing their backs, oversize jumpers pulled down over bare knees. A boy called Slug jumped into the fire once and, balancing drunkenly, danced on a burning log till his shoes and trousers singed. Sometimes the smooth lake stones which edge the fire split and crack and hot rock slivers rain down and burn small holes in their hair and skin and clothes.

On those bonfire nights, it seems to Rainey there are always shooting stars, a Milky Way so clear and vast it seems to tick. Rainey isn't sure whether anyone else notices the stars. None of them ever look up. Does Edie notice?

A speedboat passes with a roar. Edie leaps up and begins to hurl stones at it. Waves from its wake reach the shore, crashing with minor urgency. The illusion that the lake is ice is lost.

Rainey is glad she didn't know Edie when they were younger, that they didn't meet at kindergarten or primary school. The result of Edie's curiosity (what Rainey thinks of as The Edie Effect) leads to things, people even, getting broken.

Edie is the kind of person who can get by without talking.

At the moment, she is trying to build a castle of silver

river gravel in the open space between her legs and does not seem worried when, time and again, it slips and falls, escaping her design.

'I tried to have it off with Jay last night.' Edie scoops two palmfuls of gravel skywards.

'Oh.' Rainey drops the pinecone she has been examining. 'How did it go?'

'It didn't work. He said I was too tight.'

Rainey tries to look at Edie. Edie stands and stamps the piled-up gravel flat.

'Let's go for a swim,' says Edie.

'We haven't got our togs.'

'Let's go in our clothes.'

'All right.'

Strands of the wig peep out beneath the buttons of Edie's overalls. She hurls them aside. Underneath she wears a small white tee shirt and yellow velvet shorts.

In the shallows, the stones are coated in soft, slippy sludge the colour of milky coffee. They wade out to the edge of the underwater plateau, where the proper deep begins. The water's cold. It's always cold. Even during the hottest summer, only the top few inches ever warm.

'After you.'

'No, after you.'

'You first, Miss Lorraine. As you're my guest.'

'My dearest Edith, you're too kind. But truly, after you.'

Edie tries to shove Rainey. They fall, arms locked, screaming. Rainey opens her eyes, breaks the surface, sees Edie scrambling up, arms whirring, throwing the black water up so it cracks to rainbow splinters in the sun. And then Edie crouches, reaching her arms below the surface, pulling up a glass bottle half filled with mud.

Edie looks at it intently as Rainey paddles towards her.

'Jay told me I should practise with a bottle.'

'Ew. That's gross.' The bottle's clear glass is besmirched with gunge. 'Jay is such a gripper.'

'You're right, Rainey. He is a gripper.'

'You should tell him.'

'What?'

'That he's a gripper.'

'Maybe I will. I'm going to see him again tonight.'

'Don't, Edie. Please don't. Don't see him again tonight.'

Back ashore, Edie grabs her overalls and speeds into the trees. Rainey sits dripping on top of a fallen branch. The water has made her hair heavy, but she knows that when it dries it will feel soft, that it will carry in every strand a scent of ancient, alpine rock. The water has turned her white shorts transparent. The material clings to her dark blue knickers, and she thinks that perhaps Edie had planned it all, this humiliation, but then she thinks, *No, Edie wouldn't. Why would she?*

When Edie steps from the green-black shadow—back in the overalls, her wet, white tee shirt turbaning her hair—it's as if a practical sort of goddess, a hitherto unknown goddess of vehicle maintenance, Mekanike, has emerged from the grove of pines.

Edie lifts the bike and holds the handlebars.

'Come on,' she says, 'jump on. I'll push.'

'Edie,' Rainey says. 'Let's not go back.'

'It's all right, Rainey. It's not as far as you think.'

'I don't want to go back,' says Rainey.

'Yes,' says Edie. 'Yes, you do. And Rainey?'

'Yes?'

'Don't worry. It's okay. I won't see him tonight.'

Edie starts to push and the bike rolls forward. Rainey, balancing on the saddle, hears a spluttering sound. Edie's face is clenched, her mouth twisted.

'Are you crying, Edie?'

'God, no. Don't be stupid. I'm laughing.'

'Why?'

'Because I left it there.'

'Left what?'

'That stupid bloody bottle. Under the pine tree. In the place we're supposed to meet.'

The bike wobbles and Rainey falls, landing on her knees. Stones and broken bits of cone bite into her skin.

'Ow,' says Rainey. 'Ow, ow, ow.'

Edie whoops, a long, triumphant sound.

'Edie?'

'What is it, Rainey?'

'Where's the wig?'

'Damn it. Oh, goddamn it, Rainey. Don't you know I loved that wig?'

Later, when the lake is dark and the stars pour milkily across the sky, Rainey returns to the point. Even though it's night, it won't be hard to find a thing so pale. For her, it will shine as if from an inward light. And when she places it on her hair, newly close-cropped to her scalp by Edie in the late afternoon, it will make a perfect fit.

∗ A Bird So Rare ∗

THE HOTEL'S INTERIOR DÉCOR—the wood panelling in the dining room, the columns in the atrium, the startlingly beautiful carved mantelpiece in the bar—seemed charming at first glance. But as they sat down to afternoon tea, they noticed holes in the panelling on either side of the door revealing not, as they would have expected, an authentic heart of old oak beneath a time-grimed surface but hairy strands of yellow fibreglass.

'Seeing that yellow is a little death,' Frieda said. She was beginning to doubt if the two male angels guarding the fireplace, which despite their benign expressions had hands ready to draw swords from sheaths, were the real thing either. When she had first seen those angels, she had wanted to run her fingers over their dark bronze curls. Now she was glad that she hadn't, that the illusion of finding some rare treasure had lingered a little longer than it would otherwise have done, that she hadn't made a spectacle of herself and given an audience to her disappointment.

'Does it matter, though?' Michael said. 'What difference does it make whether they're real or not?'

'It makes all the difference in the world. Better if the walls were painted white. The rooms left empty. Look at them. They're beautiful rooms.'

'Yes. Yes, they are.'

The ceilings were at least twenty feet high. French doors set into bay windows opened onto a terrace that looked over the sea of trees to the coast. In the far corner of the sands, the chimneys of the china clay works gleamed silver. They were a couple of what the locals called blow-ins, people who'd drifted westwards from upcountry and stayed put. They'd been married for longer than that though, almost twenty-five years. They had met when young and stayed together while all around them, one by one, their friends' marriages and partnerships broke down. *What's your secret?* people asked them, but in truth there was no secret. They simply abided. Recently they'd had a bad patch. No particular reason; many small grievances had accumulated, each one cobweb light until they had found themselves either with nothing to say to each other or shouting and slamming doors. This holiday was their chosen salve, agreed upon because they both liked walking and, on hot days, swimming in the cold, green sea.

On the way back to their room, they stopped by a board in the foyer displaying captioned photographs of rare types of plants and animals found, over the years, in the hotel woods and gardens: strange moths, rare butterflies, enormous unidentified grubs. The grounds of the house had an oddness to them, a forgotten air, as though time itself had somehow stalled halfway down this valley. Through the open doors, the voices of families echoed as they moved to the lodges scattered throughout the trees, and somewhere a group of sea shanty singers bellowed, their voices rising to the top floor and drifting in the open window to where Frieda lay afloat, footsore after their long walk, in a tepid bath.

By the time they made their way back downstairs, the singers were gone, the early evening barbeque packed away. Dodman Point lay white in the evening light. The waters of the bay, violet with late sun, were empty of boats. Arm in arm they walked from the terrace down past an organic vegetable patch and a butterfly garden before stopping by an enclosure containing half a dozen giant rabbits, surrounded by a fence too low to be any serious attempt to contain them.

'Look at them.' Michael gestured to the huge bodies. 'Natural born killers, each and every one.'

She knew what he meant but chose to pretend not to understand him. 'You fear for your safety? Aren't rabbits herbivores? Anyway, they're all asleep. Do you think we're allowed to go in and pet them?'

'Do you *want* to go in and pet them?' Michael folded his arms.

'No, actually. No, I don't.'

'The *size* of them. They're bigger than your average cat. One bite could take your finger off.'

He was right in a way. There *was* something disturbing about them, apart from their size. Was their lethargy a result of overbreeding? In her mind rabbits were small, quick, darting little things, masters of camouflage, barely glimpsed before they'd disappeared.

'What's wrong with this place? Why can't they have normal rabbits?'

'I've no idea.'

Though Michael's eyes remained fixed on the enclosure and didn't roam to the trees, she became aware that his focus had moved on. About him was a certain intensity of concentration, a quality of stillness, his head tilted over to one side, his body poised on the edge of sudden action. He had tuned in to something calling, sweet and high, in the darkening leaves. If she spoke to him now, he would not hear what she said, so she whispered, 'Perhaps it's time we gave this up.'

When a few moments later he said, 'What was that?' she thought that perhaps she had been wrong, that he had indeed heard her, before realising that it was not she who was present in his thoughts. He was speaking of the bird which, unseen among the leaves, its call too brief to allow identification, had eluded him.

How does it feel, she silently asked the rabbits, to live with someone whose mind is always partly elsewhere, on whatever winged thing is within sight or sound? This time, the familiar anger fixed itself into a resolution. *If he does this to me one more time, I will leave him*. She was tired of arguing about it. Her mind flashed back to the time when she had been relating a piece of particularly bad news and his first comment had been, *Look, woodpecker*. She had grown used to his exclaiming suddenly, breaking off in the middle of a conversation to run to the window, realising now that it was not a sign of danger or distress but that the alarm calls of the rooftop gulls had alerted him to the flight of some raptor over the back garden. She felt no more for birds than she did for any other living things she liked, otters, for example, or hedgehogs. If forced to choose a favourite bird, she would probably pick the owl, symbol of wisdom and death, the good it promised inseparable from the evil it bestowed, as double-edged as the old gods of Mexico.

During dinner, the woman sitting at the table opposite them kept her pink iPhone raised to her face; a black eye shape on its back surrounded the camera lens. Even while she was eating, she moved the lens around the room as if she were filming everything. At another table a man, loud voiced, complained bitterly that though he'd been the second person to book a table for dinner, he hadn't been given one of a pair of window seats, haranguing the couple seated there, telling them that they had taken his place. Outside it was dark, and the doors had been closed against the evening chill.

'Busy tonight,' Michael said, not seeming to notice that they had barely spoken to each other since they had left the rabbit enclosure.

'These must be all the people we could hear earlier: the people in the trees. The room is completely full.'

'Yes,' Michael said, 'they couldn't squeeze anyone else in if they tried.'

So it was strange, the next morning, when they came down for breakfast, to find the dining room, but for themselves, completely empty. Inside her was a kind of clarifying calmness, the sort that comes, for better or worse, after a decision, long postponed, has finally been made. Now, when the moment came, all that was left for her to do was to act.

They chose a table beside the window. Morning light brightened the tops of the trees though the valley still lay in shade. The doors were open again and in drifted the smell of cut grass, green and soothing, mingling with the earth smell of the cooked mushrooms on her plate. As she raised her cup to her lips and sipped, the coffee's bitter milkiness began to warm and wake her. The sea seemed closer than it had done last night, but the black shapes of birds visible on its surface were safely distant, rising and falling with the waves' breath.

Michael began to glance repeatedly out of the window and back again. He took his glasses off and cleaned them on the thick, white linen napkin. It had come sooner than she had expected. She eased her knife and fork together on her plate, her appetite lost.

'What is it that you see?'

'What does it look like to you?' He pointed to the sparse top of a conifer, a naked looking branch almost devoid of needles. The apex. It was the exact place on their Christmas tree where she always balanced the angel.

Caught in a net of light, a bird.

'Whatever it is,' she said, 'it's big. And it looks...golden.'

'Hmmm.'

A name came into her mind along with the image of a bird so rare that she had never thought to see one in her lifetime. As big as a thrush, the bird in the tree was motionless; its yellow plumage was black edged, as if it had been carved from some dark wood and then, held delicately by its wings and tail, dipped in gilt.

'An oriole?' she said.

'It looks like one, but they're incredibly elusive. They don't just sit in trees out in the open like that.'

'This one does.'

'I can't be sure unless I go outside. Take a closer look.' He pushed his chair back.

'Michael...'

'What?'

'Michael, there's something we should...'

'What's the matter? You don't mind, do you?'

'Before you go, I think that we need to...' Across the path of her words, a shadow fell and what she had meant to say was lost in darkness. Long ago, she had read something about that ancient world of incessant substitutions, of weird metamorphoses. She had read that after his longest pursuit, in the sea off Rhamnus in Attica, Zeus had finally caught up with Nemesis: in the form of a swan, he had settled on her wild duck.

'What is it, Frieda?'

Greek mythology had once been a passion of hers, but it was a love that, with the passing of time, she had lost. The older she grew, the stranger the world seemed, increasingly hard to comprehend as it was, let alone when it was covered in layers of leaky, elaborate myth.

'It's nothing,' she said. 'Nothing's the matter. I don't mind. Go on. Off you go.'

He walked out of the doors and along the grey slabs of the terrace.

When she felt ready, pushing back her chair, she went outside and stood beside him. In flagrant defiance of the writers of bird-watching guides, the bird still sat at the top of the tree, exactly where they had first seen it.

'Well?' she said.

'I can't be sure without looking at it through binoculars.'

'You go and get them. I'll keep an eye on her for you.'

'If it is an oriole, it probably is a female. The males are more intensely golden.'

'Is that so?'

'Yes. Although as they age females become almost as bright as the males.'

'Really' she said. 'That's good to know.'

The moment after he'd stepped off the terrace, the bird took flight. Down she swooped, back into the cover of the top canopy, the place where she and her kind were known to cower; the place where, despite their extravagant colouring, they habitually eluded detection by even the sharpest-eyed of observers.

It took her a moment to register the change, her speed and grace as she skimmed through dappled forest light then up and out into the vast, unbroken blue. The next time she looked down, he was already far below her.

✳ Over the Dam ✳

'WHAT'S TAKING HER so long?' Amy's father revved the engine. Even in the shade of the carport the heat reached them, making the bare flesh on Amy's legs stick to the vinyl of the car seat. Her dad thumped the palm of his hand on the horn, so it made a strangled beep. 'What can she possibly be *doing* in there?'

'She does this every time. Every single time we go anywhere.'

Amy's mother sat in the back next to her, so that when Aunty Bea finally, as Dad would say, graced them with her presence, Bea would sit in the bucket seat, next to him, in the front.

'That's it.' Dad slammed the stick shift on the steering wheel into reverse. 'I'm not waiting any longer.'

The car shot up the driveway, raising a cloud of white dust, breath of glaciers, which puffed in through the open window and settled lazily, Amy saw, on the fine hairs coating her arm. The back of Amy's neck, damp with sweat, prickled; she shifted her hair so that it fell over her shoulder. As her dad turned towards the road, Aunty Bea appeared, blinking, handbag clutched to her stomach, pulling the door closed behind her.

'Do you want me to lock it, Gordon?' Bea's voice, like her, was reedy. She rummaged in her bag. 'I'll have to go back in for my key.'

'*Sheißen wieder,*' Amy's father said, turning off the engine and pulling the keys from the ignition.

'Don't swear, Gordon,' Amy's mum said.

'Run down and lock the door, Amy.'

Bea stepped out of the carport, taking small step after small step, looking around her as if bewildered, patting at her too-neat hair. By the time Amy had locked the door, Bea had settled into the front and was trying and failing to engage her seatbelt.

As Dad fired the engine and roared off, Bea said, 'Hold on a minute, Gordon. I can't get my belt in.'

At the end of the road, Dad stopped and leaning over Bea, yanked her seatbelt strap and slotted it into place with a loud click.

'Thank you, Gordon. Where are we going again?' Bea asked.

'I told you. To the nursery. To pick up the tree.'

'Which tree?'

'The ash tree.'

'There's no need to shout, Gordon. I was only asking you a civil question.'

God alone knew what took Aunty Bea so long to get ready to go out anywhere, even for a Sunday afternoon drive. God alone also knew what Bea did every evening, when she locked herself into the one and only bathroom to prepare her nun-smooth face for bed. Presumably Aunty Bea knew, too, but Amy sensed she should not point this fact out to her father.

'What on earth does she find to do in there?' Dad asked Amy's mother. But Amy's mother did not reply, as she often did not reply to the questions her husband or daughter asked her.

'Let's just get going, shall we? I've been meaning to collect this tree for ages.'

Other families went out at the weekend to swim in the lake or to picnic by the river. Other families went on walks, or to the swimming pool, or to playgrounds, football pitches, tennis courts. Amy's family took garden rubbish to the dump. Though it was blazing summer, they filled empty potato sacks with pinecones and pine needles, stacking them in the cool of the garage for the winter fire. They went to plant nurseries to look at plants which they would need when the rubble was finally cleared away and the garden was no longer a building site. They went to furniture showrooms to look at antiques which might, one day, fill the empty rooms of the new house.

Stunning heat fell on the little town; the lake was a blue plate, the mountains weirdly still. And the smell of them, the mountains, in the air, old and fierce and mineral. Dry grass, crushed thyme, dark pines, the gravelly margins of the road unrolling as the car moved over it, tarmac melting at its fringes. No other cars on the road. Everyone else was at the lakeshore, beneath the willows, or swimming in the bowl of fallen sky.

What day was it? All the holiday days were the same. Hot and bright and then, in the late afternoon, a breeze would rise. Amy would lie in the shade, feeling the earth beneath the rough grass pulse with heat. Tomorrow, yesterday, the moment before or after this one impossible to imagine.

They drove for a quarter of an hour or so, to another lake, edged by hills which held no summer snow. On those slopes even the grasses which covered the ground like a pelt of gold petered out, leaving barren, boulder-pitted slopes. This lake had been dammed, the water level artificially lowered. Amy had heard her parents talking about it. The false level caused erosion to undercut the shore so that great clouds of dust formed and lingered over the little town. The place had about it the bleakness of something long dead, like the body of a rat Amy had found once, fur and teeth intact but the rest dried out, shrivelled, all moisture lost.

And then they were driving over the dam, a stretch of straight, smooth road, the lake water glass on one side of them and on the other, at the end of a long, grassed slope, a roaring narrow outlet, whitely churning, and then a river, a strangely opaque green river, snaking homewards, out of sight.

The nursery was in the back blocks, one of the many identical sections surrounded by conifer hedges. At first it appeared to be deserted, aside from a lone red dog barking at a wire fence.

'There's a sign on the fence, Gordon,' Aunty Bea said. 'Lakeland Nursery. I wonder if it's closed.' But then a man came out of the house, sullenly rubbing his eyes.

'Are you not open today?' Amy's father stepped out of the car.

'Yes, we're open.' But still he seemed puzzled to see them.

As the man opened the gate, the dog came up and circled Amy. A dry fear gripped her throat.

'There's no need to cry,' her mother said. 'He won't bite you.'

Had no one else seen the dog bare its teeth? Had no one else heard its low growl?

'Stupid mutt. Stop that.' As the man grabbed the dog by the collar and dragged it off, it began to slash the air with its teeth.

By the time Amy had licked some tears off the corner of her mouth, rubbing the rest away with the back of her hand, her parents and Aunty Bea had walked on, past row after row of parched saplings wilting in polythene bags.

'A golden ash,' Amy's father said. 'I ordered it...when was it? Last year?'

'And you paid?'

'Yes. But the garden wasn't ready then. So I said I'd be back.'

A hose dripped on the ground, wetting the light brown earth, turning it black. In the farthest corner, where two lengths of windbreak met, the man tried to tug a bagged tree out of a cluster.

'This is it,' the man said, 'but it's more than twelve months since you bought it. It was years ago.'

'Perhaps it was.' As the sun fell on Amy's father, it seemed to make him transparent, to drain him of life, of colour. 'Sometimes it takes longer than you think.'

'To do what?'

'To get back.'

Turning away from them, the man began to tug again at the tree.

What if you don't? Amy wanted to ask. *What if you never get back? What happens if you never get back?* And if the dog was locked up, how come she could feel its hot breath, hear the rumble of warning rising in its throat?

'That tree doesn't look very healthy, Gordon.' Aunty Bea's light voice quavered. 'Has it got some disease?'

Its leaves were deformed, their tips stuck to the leaf stems as if they had been interrupted in the middle of opening.

'Pot bound. That's the trouble.' The man tipped the bag to the side, ripping loose yellow-white roots grown out of the plastic and into the ground. 'It won't thrive.'

'I'll tease the roots out.'

'That'll help. But still. I can't guarantee it. You might have left it too long.'

'Well,' Amy's father said, 'let's take it to the car.'

Despite being stunted, the tree was too large to fit into the boot. In the end, they squeezed it into the foot well of the front passenger seat where its bent crown brushed the roof.

Aunty Bea climbed into the back beside Amy. As they pulled away, Amy could hear the dog barking, barking. She saw the man let it out of the house, saw it throw itself against the fence so hard the wire juddered. Her hands were cold despite the heat, so she squashed them beneath her thighs. And then, as they began to cross the dam, a motorcycle screamed up and tore past them.

'Oh,' Aunty Bea gasped, 'what a madman. Do be careful, Gordon.'

'He'll kill himself,' Amy's father said, and at that moment the bike wobbled and, slipping to the side of the dead straight road, spun over the edge, the black clad man and the machine disappearing, quicker than a blink, over the bank.

'Stop, Gordon. Quick, stop.'

'Of course I'm going to stop.'

Down the long, too-smooth-to-be-natural slope, Amy saw the black figure. He had fallen perhaps two-thirds of the way, stopping just before the lip of the outlet pipe, the wild cascade of white water. Now he stood and, after wobbling a little, began to climb, the helmet still in place on his head, the weight of his body tipped forward onto his hands against the slope. The bike was caught on the gravel of the soft shoulder. There was a dull roar Amy thought was the sound of water being forced through the narrow channel, the great weight of water from the huge dark lake, the lake stretching up to those snowless peaks, but it was not that, it was not water, because when her father walked down to the bike and turned its engine off the noise stopped. And then her father waited, arms crossed, for the climbing man to reach the road. As soon as the rider stepped over the brink, Amy's father shouted, 'You idiot! Why were you driving so fast? You could have killed us as well as yourself.'

'Fuck off.' The man, failing in his attempt to lift the bike, let it drop. 'Just piss on out of it.' After kicking the bike's undercarriage, helmet still on, he began to walk down the middle of the road back in the direction of the town.

Amy's father got back in the car. For a moment he just sat there, his hands opening and closing on the steering wheel.

No one said anything, not even Aunty Bea.

Why hadn't her father asked the man if he were hurt? Why hadn't her father asked him if he needed any help? Light slanted in the front windscreen, catching in the branches of the golden ash, which shuddered gently as the car began to move. Why *were* they going home to plant a tree that, even if it managed to survive, would never thrive? And though a few moments later they passed over the dam and were driving along the road that would lead them back to the new house, why could she not shake off the feeling that they were somehow lost, that they were now travelling in entirely the wrong direction, that they were on their way to anywhere but home.

* Like Leaves *

JOHNNY'S NOT THE FIRST UP, not by any means. Since the hunting season began, the rumble of cold, protesting engines breaks the stillness long before dawn. Up on the mountains, in the trackless forests, on the swampy edge of tarns, on the bitter white shores of the lake's far reaches, guns are being loaded, aim taken. Though it's too distant for the sound to carry, he sometimes wakes in the darkness and thinks he's heard it, the crack of shots splintering the air.

The timeshares and hotel units are long and low, half hidden by carefully planted birches and constructed grassy slopes so that, though the lake shore path is close by, you don't see them till you're amongst them. Johnny has thought about this many times, the tricks of sight that allow the resort to hide the way it does, in landscaped folds. It's the lawn that gives the game away, the unnatural greenness of it too obvious a contrast from the rough, surrounding golden grasses and the coarse, silver gravel of the shore.

Inside the main building, split lake stones are stacked to make a fireplace big enough to stand in; the roof is high and wood panelled. Steps lead down to bar and the Fish Bowl beyond. Pam is on reception and Lenny's leaning over the counter, shouting something at her while she tries to type. Lenny's a groundsman who prides himself on doing as little as possible. Johnny raises his hand and flashes his badge and keeps walking when Lenny says, 'Just a minute there, Johnno'.

Johnny pretends he hasn't heard. He pushes through the swing doors and enters the staff area. The corridor is cold and windowless. A line of fluorescent strips lights the low ceiling, illuminating the concrete floor, the breeze block walls. It's always a shock, the contrast between all the glass and light outside and this barren warren. In the housekeeper's room, Mag sits behind her desk. A baby blue angora jersey, home-knitted, bags over her tunic and a matching scarf is wrapped so high around her throat it covers her chin. In front of her, a teacup of white liquid—half milk and half hot water—holds down the day's rota.

'Busy today, Mag?' Johnny puts his jacket in his locker but doesn't bother closing the door. A key to replace the lost one is another job Lenny's been meaning to get round to for years.

'Not too bad, Dor. I've put you on rooms till eleven. You can restock the minibars after smoko.'

Dor is Mag's pet name for him, a shortened form of Dorian. She says he never looks any older. If anything, he's getting younger by the day. She says he has an evil pact with a portrait he keeps stashed in his attic, though he's told her more than once that he doesn't have an attic. As he bends to buff the white dust from his shoe tips, an outside smell rises from it, the mineral scent of powdered stone.

'Oh, Mag. Not minibars. Not again.'

Mag smiles, a little. It's a soft job compared to stripping beds and cleaning baths, dusting and luxing. Only Mag's favourites get minibars.

The other cleaners, all women but for him, drift in, move around the room, filling their trolleys with clean sheets and towels, soaps and sachets of tea, coffee, sugar and miniature bottles of the fresh milk Mag insists on. Sometimes he teases her, says she only does it so she can hoard the dregs to make her pale brew.

Hurry is for other places, not here: that's what Johnny feels as he opens the door to the first vacant unit. This place is for quietness, for resting, not rushing. Just sit and look at the mountains and the lake and you'll see it, you'll feel it. Along the lakefront, willows and poplars are losing their green to the creep of red, orange, yellow. *Unmasking*, Bobby called it, the chlorophyll shrinking back to expose the true colours beneath. Autumn is the tearing away of disguises.

Even this early in the morning, many of the visitors have departed for excursions. All manner of noisy activities are on offer unless the weather closes in. Hard to believe it, looking at the placid lake, the eerie stillness of the mountains, but Johnny has seen storms powerful enough to frighten him break over these peaks—torrential rain and snow, thunder and lightning and howling gales screaming in on the tail of an afternoon nor'wester even after the gentlest of mornings.

What's the hurry, Bobby always used to say. *Calm down a little bit, why don't you?*

Johnny closes the door, leaning back against it for a moment to stop and look and listen, to let the light settle. The sun's creeping round now, crossing the gravel shore and the lip of the lake, hitting the tops of the highest peaks. A moment ago, the snow was blue; as he watches, the light turns it faintly buttery before brightening it to white.

What's the hurry?

Johnny slides open the glass door.

The slightest, softest breeze, the drop of a pinecone onto a bed of needles, a chill edge of approaching winter, stone mountain cold in the air.

Seeing the departed guests spoils the game. He prefers to search for traces, however subtle. Which have they chosen—coffee or tea? Are they messy or clean? Most do okay in the bedroom and living room, but the bathrooms can still surprise him. Even towels that haven't been used tend to have been interfered with, thrown or let fall in the shower tray, on the floor. A waste, he thinks gathering them up. What a waste.

He squirts the bath with Jif and scrubs it, then runs some water, scalding hot, into the hand basin. After stripping the linen from the beds, he dips the corner of a pillowcase in the water and rubs it on the mirror, hard and fast through the steamy surface, to produce a perfect, smudge-free finish. Another of Mag's tricks, the shine it gives brighter than any spray.

Once the beds are made up, he cleans the kitchen surfaces and gets luxing; the carpet is horrible—dense, commercial grade stuff that everything sticks to. Last week, on his rounds, Swinson found a peanut under a sofa. Apocalypse. Swinson screamed the housekeeping office down and Mag got yet another cold and started dosing herself with hot, white muck.

When he is as sure as he can be that room 544 is clean and peanut-free, Johnny closes and locks the door.

In 271, spotlights pump out heat above the desk and beds. The curtains are closed, and the air is swampy. For a moment Johnny feels he's elsewhere, a hotel in a foreign city, somewhere equatorial, a place neither clean nor safe. In a wastepaper bin is a blood-stained jacket, a pair of sanguineous knives. Christ, oh Christ. What's happened here? He moves outside again, looks for help, but there's no one. He checks his hands for bloodstains but there's none, of course. They're shaking though, his hands, and his heart's crashing beneath his ribs as if turned to liquid, pounding like some fierce, red tide. He thinks of calling out but he's afraid of startling them, the guests, waking them from their holiday sleepwalk.

He scuttles back inside and lifts the phone. 'Mag?'

'What may I do for you, ever youthful one?'

'There's blood up here. Knives, with blood on them, in the room, in the bin and clothes…'

'Slow down…'

'And what if there's someone here, I mean, someone murdered?'

'Here? At Edgewater? Don't be a berk, Dor.'

'You should see it, Mag.'

'What number did you say?'

'271.'

'Businessmen in there the last few days. They went out with Ron yesterday.'

Ron with the chopper. Deer hunting. Soft, brown fur, sliced open, still warm bodies. Jesus. 'So, what do I do? What do I do with the knives?'

'Just hang on a minute. You sit tight. I'll send Lenny up.'

Lenny. Great.

Johnny's heart still beats hard enough to make his body shake. The blood is dry. Or is it? He can't be sure, that's him all over; never been sure in his life except the once. He wishes Bobby were here now, too. He thinks about getting up and turning the lights off, but he wants someone else to see what he saw when he opened the door. Lenny takes his time, the lazy bastard. Knocks but doesn't wait for an answer, opens the door with his master.

'What the…?' Lenny says.

'They were out with Ron, apparently.'

Lenny crouches down by the bin and sniffs, as if were still possible to get a scent off these objects, of beech trees and fern, of ancient stone and moss, of glacier-fresh ice and snow melt water.

'These are worth a fair bit.' Lenny looks happy, cradling the knife handle in his palm. 'Only been used the once. You want one to take home, Johnno?'

'No thanks, Len.'

'Clothing's good, too.' From under the jacket, Lenny pulls a vest with lots of little bullet-sized pockets. Abstract sprays of blood splatter it, and it's a pale, creamy colour, not even camouflage, which seems so stupid that Johnny starts laughing, though it's not a happy laugh, and Lenny looks at him, wanting him to explain, but all Johnny says is, 'Like I said. I'm right.'

Lenny slides on his gauntlets. Johnny opens the bathroom door.

'Tell you what,' Lenny says, 'even if you wash it, this bin's going to pong a bit. How 'bout I rinse it out with the power hose?'

Johnny backs out of the bathroom and turns to Lenny.

'Your face. What?' says Lenny. 'What is it?'

The bathroom is awash. The bath water is dotted with soaking towels all stained a faintish pink.

'Jeez. What a mess.'

'Lenny, is there any chance you could drop these towels to Mag? Otherwise they'll soak through my linen bag.'

'Oh, dear. We can't have *that*, can we?'

Lenny comes so close, Johnny can see the short whiskers round his nose, missed during his morning shave, the flaky redness of the skin on his chin.

'The trials of a housemaid. Okay, Johnno. Just this once. And only cos you asked so *nicely*.'

When Lenny comes back with the cleaned out bin,

Johnny hands him the half full bottle of Chivas Regal he found wrapped up, snug as a baby, in the folds of one of the duvets.

'You've struck gold today, boy. What say we have a nip?'

Lenny fills the cap and knocks it down then passes it to Johnny.

'Whoa.' The heat of it fills Johnny's mouth, a stinging, burning kiss.

'Choice stuff. Damn pricey, too. This is going to make my day a whole lot better. You wouldn't take the knives, but surely…'

'You take it. You'll enjoy it more than…I'd just like you to. Go on. You have it. Please.'

The whisky's in Johnny's veins now, filling his head with fluttering. He thinks of the time that he and Bobby walked down to the cove, a place at the head of the lake where the water's always still and deep, green-black as polished greenstone, a place sheltered by a bluff covered in viper's bugloss and pale dog roses. They'd been trying to find somewhere away from prying eyes. Tiny, slate blue butterflies rose from the shore, their underwings dust grey, hundreds and hundreds of them rose like smoke and covered their bare arms and legs and hair and then, a heartbeat later, they were gone. Bobby, who normally talked so much, didn't have a thing to say. He just shook his head and then grabbed Johnny round the waist and led him into the water.

After they'd swum, Bobby nodded out to what was opposite them, a rare piece of flat land in the midst of so many mountains. *That's the place I was telling you about. The farm where Dad sometimes makes me go.*

To do what?

Learn stuff. Like how to shear sheep. And how to slaughter them.

The way Bobby'd described it, it sounded weird, sacrificial. And his father made him do other things too, like fell trees and climb mountains and raft down rivers. Always trying to toughen him up.

The sun is full on the lake now. The sound of voices rises to the open window, along with the drone of a light plane taking off into the blue. Eleven o'clock, Johnny guesses, the time when he's usually close to finishing his round, the time when hunters come home from the hills. He's three units behind. Mag will have given minibars to one of the others.

There.

Gone.

All gone.

The bloody clothes and knives and towels, the fug of cigar smoke, the tang of whisky, all swept and tidied away, washed clean again. The next guests in 271 will never know.

He opens the bathroom window a fraction and sprays some air freshener around before locking the door.

By the time he gets back to Mag's bunker, it's past one.

'What a morning.'

'You going to eat?' Mag is dipping a cracker into a bowl of soup.

'Have I got time?'

'Go on, Dor. You're too skinny.'

In the canteen, Lenny, at a table with other ground staff, winks at Johnny. A new friend for life. After what happened to Bobby, Johnny tries to stay off the booze, to keep his head clear. *Tonight,* he thinks, a trace of whisky burning a tiny candle in his chest, *I'll light the fire and drink some beer. Or red wine, maybe.* Nights are cold this time of year, as soon as the sun goes down, and always the curve of mountains waiting, holding the chill blue air cupped in their palms.

Johnny carries his tray back to eat with Mag but she's on the phone, her glove-clad fingers pulling at her scarf. Swinson, giving her another earful. Johnny wonders what it is this time and whether she'll leave this job, this place. Leave him. That's the trouble with making your heaven on earth with rough materials, with other people's scraps and leftovers. It can all be swept away so easily.

Mag offers Johnny a lift home, but he says no. He doesn't head along the lakeshore this time but out along the road, over the stile and up the old avenue of lime trees, so close planted that their top foliage is bound up together; in the summer, their sticky, pale green buds drop down and tangle in his hair. Now the leaves, a light, lemony yellow and almost translucent, are falling, a great, tender carpet of them. Not many people know about this place. Most of the time, he's the only one here.

Beyond the avenue is a garden, borders of rhododendrons and camellias. An old archway, covered in roses, leads nowhere, and amongst it all are the foundations of a homestead burnt down long ago. On the grass lies an empty beer bottle and a playing card, the two of hearts.

Snap, says Bobby. *You lose. Not very good at this, are you?*

Johnny climbs the steps up to where the front door once stood. Nothing there now but air. On one side of him is a bronze plaque engraved with the original architect's drawing of the vanished house. On his other side, sweet-scented mauve roses with golden stamens bloom. Lavender bushes, their flowers past, hold dry husks on dying stalks. The sun's warm, and there's a little breeze, the slight kind there was this morning but warm and soft now, so soft. It's only later, when some people come up the lake path that Johnny remembers he's by himself, because he doesn't feel alone. The people are looking at him. Looking away. They've heard him talking to Bobby and he doesn't want them to worry so, though he'd like to stay longer, he walks on.

The sun's getting lower, lighting up the grasses, turning the end of the day as golden as the morning was. At New World, Johnny buys eggs and bread and mushrooms and butter and a bottle of red. On the way up the hill, a car slows beside him and through the open window, Lenny says, 'Thanks again for the Chivas. Ted Baker says he'll give us one-fifty for the knives, but... Stop walking and listen to me, boy. I'm saying you should keep one. Never know when it might come in handy.'

'No thanks, Lenny.' The plastic carrier bag is cutting into Johnny's palm, so he rests it down in the soft, white dust at his feet. 'You take them both. To keep or sell, whatever you like.'

'Never go hunting?'

'Not me.'

'What's wrong with you, boy?'

I'm a vegetarian, Lenny. You see me in the canteen with my lunch tray every day. And you've never noticed. 'You keep them, Lenny. The knives. The jackets, too. I don't want them. You keep the money.'

'You sure? You really mean it? Good lad. You're a good lad. I don't care what they say about you.'

'Okay. Well. I'd better be...'

'Tell you what, then. I'll make you a deal. You ever need a hand with anything, anyone ever gives you any trouble, you let Lenny know.'

'Will do.'

'Sure you don't want a lift, son?'

'I'm sure.'

'All right, then. And another thing. I wanted to say... don't you worry, boy. Things'll come right for you. Give it time.'

'Thanks, Lenny. I... Goodness. I appreciate it. Right, then. Cheerio.'

The car's tail lights, ember bright, make Johnny realise dusk has come. He puts his head down, allowing himself a little smile until he sees Lenny brake outside the Fish Hatchery and start reversing.

'I forgot to say. He's coming.'

'Who?'

'That fella you like.'

A moment of arrhythmic hope. 'You don't mean...'

'What's his name? That poet.'

Of course, it wasn't Bobby. How could it be Bobby?

'You okay? You've gone a funny colour. That's twice today.'

'When will he be here? The poet, I mean.'

'Can't remember exactly. Sometime in the next few days. That's what I was trying to tell you this morning. You make sure to keep a look out.'

At home, Johnny pulls down the kitchen blinds. Round here, if they see lights on, people take it as an invitation to drop in for a visit. Last thing he needs is Lenny showing up again. The fire's already laid so Johnny sets a match to it and sits on the floor with the sofa at his back. He's tired, finally, which is what he aims for, a deep fatigue that will sail him over dark water and into tomorrow before he knows it.

The poet had last come three years ago in this same season: the time of falling leaves, of drift, of sun's retreat and snow's advance. They let the poet bring his dog into the bar, a border collie with mismatched eyes. *Those dogs aren't pets*, someone said and, leaning towards Johnny, Bobby whispered about how, up on the farm at the top of the lake, he'd seen them beat the sheepdog pups with lengths of hosepipe. *To train them*, Bobby said, and his dark fringe fell forward and into his eyes. Most of the waiting staff had turned out because the poet didn't start performing till service was over. They were sitting on a sofa together in front of the fire, Johnny and Bobby, nineteen years old, waiters at Edgewater.

The poet was an artful mess. Cowboy boots and black stovepipes and flannel shirt and electric shock hair. Johnny liked the way he worked the words, the banter—about the boatshed he lived in and how he swung in his hammock above the water when spring tides flooded it—and then in the interval he put a tape on. A woman was singing a song about passionate kisses and he and Bobby looked at each other and knew.

Johnny'd thought a lot about it since, the way that poet stood up there and put on a performance every night. And about something he'd said. Johnny can't remember the exact words. Something like *gentleness is not a lack of strength*, a phrase that Bobby would sometimes repeat.

It had been a beautiful morning, as clear and calm as this one. Bobby and his father had been stalking for a few hours. Bobby's father said he thought his son was behind him but when he looked around, he couldn't see him. He called and shouted and waited and, when the chopper came for the pickup, Ron helped him search but they found nothing. Not a single trace. And then, over the mountains and the head waters, the weather closed in.

Half the wine is gone. Johnny should get up and feed the fire, cook some mushrooms and scramble some eggs. He tries not to fixate, to read something into the day's events—the bloody clothes and knives in the wastepaper bin, Lenny and the whisky and the return of the poet.

Bobby told him that there's no soil on the mountains. Trees cling on to sheer rock, twining their roots around each other, and on them grow lichens and mosses and algae, and beneath them shrubs and ferns and fungi, all of it woven together on a bed of millions of fallen leaves.

Out there, in the bush, keep to the marked route at all costs, that's what Johnny was taught at school. Never stray. In the places Bobby and his father went, the only tracks are those left by the passing of boar and deer. The trees repeat, endless permutations of southern beech and totara, kahikatea and tree fern, indistinguishable from one another once you enter. Wander off the path and, in the time it takes to blink, the bush will turn you round.

Now the wine's running through him and the days with Bobby fall through his mind, leaf after leaf, same seeming but each one different. The days and the hours, the minutes and the seconds live in him still. All he needs to do is what he's already doing: to carry on, to stand and wait. And then, like Bobby, he'll see a path opening out before him, and he'll think, perhaps it's time to follow it. Follow it to the very end.

* La Crue de la Seine *

THE RIVER RISING THROUGH the old quarries, the underground galleries of golden limestone, signs of the flood on our pediments.

A bend in the river, and now the water's too slow, with all these islands, with all these bridges, and so it rises; its dirty line stains us

(around every river is an unseen river)

breaking free, breaking out of its walls, its channels broken

You: *We'll be safe on the third floor* but I'm not so sure, no I'm not so sure

The cries of the flower sellers beneath the horse chestnuts and the white lilac forced. It should not be white. It should be, well, lilac. It should be, well, lilac

and also peonies, the right colour peonies, and also violets

in the park that man picked a pigeon up, and cuddled and stroked it, his bed rolled behind him, that man picked a pigeon up

these *glaces* like flowers, each petal moulded with that strange little implement, half knife and half spoon—*au chocolat, à la fraise, à la menthe*—

by the Tuileries path, a garden disappearing; two box hedges, spiralling, the height of the hedges and the flowers diminishing until both descend *souterrain* as if into the underworld.

Do you see? How clever whoever designed it, how terribly, terribly clever

and the room like an eye, all curves and water, silver and grey, grey and silver, the band of water and the floating flowers and the shadows of the trees and the light sent back so you've no idea what's beneath it, that dark grey water

and you feeding crumbs to sparrows which rested on your hand, and the man dressed in green, Granny Smith top hat and lichen shirt and grass green waistcoat, malachite trousers and moss green shoes and chestnut cane with a bright gold top; did you see the man dressed in green?

Upstairs, the red curtains (I laughed when first I saw them) don't seem so funny, no, they don't seem so funny. In the stone sink, I put wine in to cool and then sit by the window and look down on top hats, the careful, circular nap of their crowns so many universes, so many black holes.

Where are you?

Never here when you're needed.

Never here when you're needed.

* Error *

MATILDA HAD RUNG SO EARLY it was still night to say that they wouldn't be coming to visit after all. The baby was on its way and they were at the hospital. Things were progressing but slowly.

'And everything's okay, is it?'

'Yes, but I've a feeling it's going to be a long labour. The first time can be hardest.'

He'd gone back to the bed then, sliding in next to Anne while Matilda's words ran through him, tugging him back every time he got close to dropping off. At last, he got up again and opened the curtains till he glimpsed the creek's shallow water. At high tide, he could kayak to the other side in five minutes and be amongst the overhanging branches of maritime beech and oak and pine and holly. The creek used to be navigable up to its highest reaches, but the defunct mine workings up the valley filled it with silt, their legacy mile after mile of mud. But the mud was beautiful, if you had an eye for it—the way it glittered after the tide went out, the way it dried in the sun, the way the birds hopped about on it, probing and turning, white egrets and godwits reflected in the mirrors of its tide pools.

Proper light was coming now, a dawn no longer the gentle rose of summer but dark gold, orange and crimson, the water beneath it flat and stony-looking, mossy green. He could hear the cattle lowing, and all the birds were calling now though they had not been silent through the night, they never were. In a moment he would get up and go out into the garden. He'd done it many times before, walked to the water's edge and watched and waited for the dawn.

Brightness was trapped behind the curtains. He'd been deep in a dream, one of those ones where you felt awake but weren't. Dreaming that he was doing something he had never done, holding the baby in his arms and singing, *La la li, la la li*.

The bi-fold doors into the garden were open but he didn't call to Anne. He carried his tea and toast outside and when he saw her look up from where she was kneeling, weeding the earth with a shiny fork, he waved and settled on the decking.

'I wouldn't have minded some.' She paused on her way to empty her trug.

'Tea? I'll make more.'

'Did you not make a pot?'

'I will this time. And toast, for you?'

'A Ryvita,' she said, 'with cottage cheese.'

'Matilda rang. They won't make it down today after all. The baby's coming early, can you believe it?'

'Goodness. Well.'

'Shall we walk the track this afternoon?'

'I've a lot to do.'

'Nothing that can't wait now that they're not coming.'

Anne clipped her secateurs shut. 'There was a message when I checked the answerphone this morning.'

'What did it say? Is everything okay?'

'It's by the phone.'

Still a way to go was written on the paper, along with the name of the hospital. He tried ringing Matilda's mobile, but she didn't answer.

With the coast path so near, they had planned to do more walking, but Anne often had other things on. He'd got used to going out alone, planning his route with a lunchtime pub stop. People said retirement was a shock. All that time together suddenly, getting on each other's nerves, but they saw less of each other than before.

Not far from their house, an underpass dived under the main road. It was always odd, crossing from the sheltered, leafy creek to a post-industrial valley almost bare of vegetation. The county was so narrow here you could walk from coast to coast in a couple of hours.

The track was wide. There was a cycle path and plenty of space for walkers, except through a couple of pinch points where wooden bridges spanned quiet streams. The sun was bright and hot in the valley, so they stopped in the shelter of the viaduct to pack away their fleeces. He asked her if she'd like a Tracker bar but she said no. Female friends would pat the ghosts of their waists and say, *Lucky Anne, no kids. See what it does to you.* And he'd found himself wanting to say, *No, it's not that, don't blame the lack of kids.*

It got more rugged the further north they went, the wide trail narrowing, zigzagging across roads, around houses, over bridges. Steel mesh cones topped old adits. More proper trees grew, birch and holm oak, along with patches of the ripest, most abundant blackberries he'd ever seen.

Just before the coast, the land dipped down between two hills. There was another main road to cross, no underpass this time, and a shabby beach in the shape of an eyelid. The arm of a quay reached out into the sea and through the sand a stream ran to the waves. A bright, noisy squadron of children were building dams in it, happy in those little wetsuits and the occasional one stark naked but for a pair of wellies or a nappy.

They sat on a battered picnic bench and ate toasted sandwiches. Anne was rubbing cream into her arms, across the back of her neck; it settled briefly on her skin before it disappeared.

'We should have brought our togs.'

'Don't be ridiculous.'

'It's not ridiculous. The sea's at its warmest now.'

'That's your phone.'

His hearing was going. It was definitely going. 'Matilda?'

He stood and wandered further down the promenade, past blow-up crocodiles, buckets, spades, those colourful windmills kids plant in the sand.

'It's a girl,' Matilda said. 'A beautiful little girl.'

'Wonderful,' he said. 'Are they both well?'

'The baby has a bit of jaundice. Saskia. That's her name.'

'What a lovely... jaundice did you say?'

'Might be a sign of infection. They'll stay in a few days at least. I'll send some photos through to your phone.'

'Imagine if it had happened here. The baby arriving. Clare was going to be here, wasn't she? Three months early, today, of all days...'

'*Rebecca*,' Matilda said, 'wanted to say sorry but she doesn't feel up to talking yet.'

Rebecca? Oh yes, that was her name now, had been her name for forty years; Clare was his name for her. Clare Violet.

'Give them my love,' he said, as the signal went.

The wind was much stronger here and he pointed his face into it, as he'd seen birds do, to clear his eyes.

As they descended back into the valley, he was struck again by its lingering sense of brokenness. All this desolation, a UNESCO World Heritage Site. Above them on the viaduct, a blue ribbon of train slid almost noiselessly south. Anne had barely spoken for an hour, maybe more.

'Let's stop for a drink. To celebrate.'

'Must we? I'm in no state to be seen.'

'You look fine. Pink-cheeked.'

'My cheeks are never pink.'

Geese flew low over the wetland. From their seat outside the pub, they watched more of them graze the soggy grass. It was a favourite spot, one that caught and kept the sun. While all around them slipped into shade they sat in their island of light, but it had never felt wrong to him before.

'Anne, you don't seem happy. I want to understand why you aren't happy for me.'

'I knew you had a life before. Of course, I did. But I didn't plan on this.'

'I thought I'd told you. That I'd explained it all when we were courting.'

'If I'd even thought it was a possibility...'

When they met, her hair was a rich, creamy brown. Now it was the colour of salt. 'Then what? What would have been different?'

She held her wine glass up searching for smudges, the marks of other lips or fingers. If she found any, she would send him back to the bar with it.

'Do you mean that you wouldn't have married me?'

'I can't say, can I? Not now.'

'Why not?'

'Because it's too late.'

He had stayed single till his early forties, though

there'd been plenty of girlfriends. Then along came beautiful Anne who wouldn't settle for less than a ring on her finger.

The years had gone. Photos filed behind plastic, the blind spines of labelled albums. How could it all be behind them? He felt it rise in him again, the terror he'd felt, the fright. Forty years ago. Matilda. Clare.

'She was so brave.'

'Who's she? You don't mean me?'

It was not true, what their parents said. They had not been careless. He and Matilda had already split up when she found out she was pregnant. Matilda's courage was unequalled. He hadn't even had the guts to go to the hospital. But he had sent flowers. Surely, he had sent flowers? All that thinking what was best for the future—what did that mean now?

'I'll get you another.'

In the pub's dark interior, he held onto to the wall. He could see Anne rubbing cream into her hands but not well enough. It would leave a mark on her glass, and then she'd make him return it. How had he never noticed it was her who made the marks?

'She's my daughter, Anne. The baby is my granddaughter.'

'They're complete and utter strangers.'

'I can't imagine it will alter our lives as much as you think it might.'

'Once you've started down that path, there's no going back. Do I not get a choice? It's not just your life it touches.'

Of course, there would be an impact. Worlds were turning on this. Legacies on lives long after his was past.

Their house was clean and bright with water light. A

dream home, Anne called it, and he hated it, hated the matching towels and the fig reed diffusers, hated the his and hers sinks in their bloody ensuite. He hated the bidet with its little gold taps that no one had ever, and probably never would, wash their arse in.

'Now she has a child of her own she wants to know me. They ask questions at the prenatal appointments. It's not something adoptive parents can *do*.'

That's why she'd got in touch after all this time. Her adoptive parents were gone from this world. She'd found her birth mother, Matilda, who passed on his details. He'd heard Clare's relief at the news his medical history was so free from incident. There was no unusual blood type, no patterns of disease through generations. It hurt him that she wanted so little, so he'd asked if she wanted to meet.

It had caused him brief anguish to lie to her. The only operation he'd had was elective. At the time, its pain level was high enough to alleviate some of his distress, nothing more than he deserved. ('Are you certain,' someone had asked him at the time, 'that this is not an act of grief?' 'Grief?' he'd said. 'What grief?') And now his granddaughter (only *technically*, Anne said) had come early. What excuses were there now? What inconvenient circumstances?

Surprising the ducks, he poured his beer into the water. 'I thought I'd drive up tonight. Stop somewhere on the road for supper.'

'You don't even know if she wants you there.'

'That doesn't matter. That really doesn't matter.'

'If you want to make a fool of yourself, go ahead. But leave me out of it.'

'Are you sure that's what you want?'

'I've never been more certain of anything.'

'All right then. As you wish.'

He waited but she did not say anything else. When her drink was finished, they walked home. After that it was simple. He set out on the long drive north.

* Tissue *

THIS MORNING I WAS spring-cleaning, wiping the muck off the inside of the windows with pieces of tissue paper gathered over time—from shoe boxes and packaging, for example—for this purpose.

(I should explain that I've not been well, have lain for the last two months in bed looking at the dust gathering on the pane, at the line where the cat rubs her nose back and forth against the glass as her eyes rake the dark garden, at the small, opaque impact marks insects leave behind them, at tiny green flowers of some algae or mould, and that fine, dark, black matter that dunes in the window's corners.)

As I wiped, I saw a word printed slantwise on the paper, denser white on pale translucency, visible against the light. The word was *POETRY*.

Over and again—*POETRY, POETRY, POETRY.*

* Flowers *

AT THE RED POST BOX, she turns down a deeply rutted lane; lumps of granite show white through its broken surface. She opens the gate, parking as instructed, then walks down a track lined with the winter white stalks of last year's grass and wildflowers.

This is the place: four fields in the shape of a rough parallelogram. Near the track, on her left, one area of the closest field is enclosed behind wire mesh. A path runs through long, wet grass towards a gate in the fence. In the bottom right-hand corner is an open-fronted barn with a caravan parked inside it, a chimney rising from its roof.

She peers into the caravan window but she cannot see anyone inside. Cold from the earth rises through the soles of her gumboots. She is about to leave when, looking again, she notices a figure kneeling inside the fencing.

She walks over but he does not seem to know she is there. He is wearing a suit, some kind of woollen weave, not tweed.

Hello.

Hello.

He is young, younger than her. He stands and wipes his hands on his clothes. His hair is flat and yellowish. Despite his smile, his face is the wrong kind of white. He has been ill. Is still ill, perhaps.

Rachel said you wanted someone to grow flowers.

Yes. He shakes his head as if confused. I was asleep. I still have to sleep a lot. But I remember now.

She doesn't know what to say. She doesn't know what she was expecting but it was not this.

Are you cold? he says. It's cold today.

And bleak, she does not say, this place is bleak.

Let's have some tea.

He washes his hands at a standpipe. The barn smells of dirt and straw, the caravan of damp. The bed is a heap of sleeping bags and blankets; the cups are stained with a thick crust of tannin. Roll-up butts huddle, crushed together in a jar lid.

Sit down. Here. He moves a pile of books from a seat. Rachel said you were a florist.

Well, yes. Sort of. I mean, I never meant to be. It wasn't what I wanted.

He lights the camp stove, rolls a cigarette.

My parents were. Florists, I mean. My grandmother started growing flowers in the Great Depression. My grandfather lost his job on the railways. Five kids and nothing to eat. She doesn't know why she is telling him this. She doesn't tell anyone this. She shakes her head.

I don't have any biscuits.

It doesn't matter.

I only have goat's milk. Is that okay?

Yes. She has never drunk goat's milk. That's okay.

After they have finished, they go out into the field. It is raining. In her mind the earth has a red tint but now she sees that, under the rain, the soil is a deep brown, black, almost. He has laid out some beds within the wire mesh, six rectangles of soil. The fence is to keep out the rabbits which will otherwise eat everything.

Look. He points to a line of feathery green leaves. I planted them in December and they're up already.

Are they a type that grows in winter?

No. I was late putting them in because I was in hospital. All this should have been done earlier, in the summer and autumn. This soil must be good soil.

It looks like good soil, but she will not know until she starts to work it. The rain is heavy now, too heavy for her to begin anything.

In the shelter of the barn, he shows her rows of tools. Most are old but some are new, their dull silver light an oddity amongst the rest, the well-used and the worn.

A few days later she drives to the post box, turns down the lane, parks on the other side of the gate. She walks down the rutted track to the field, a bin bag filled with hand tools, gloves, packets of seeds, nets of bulbs, swinging from her hand. Inside the shelter of the barn, still air that could mistakenly be called warm but is only the cessation of wind. There is no sign of him, though she scans the field for a crouched figure in a suit. She peers in the window and sees him curled up on his side, blankets and sleeping bags heaped around him, holes in the bottom of his socks.

She goes out of the barn into the fine drizzle. Climbs over the rabbit fence and puts the bin bag down by the side of the bed of freshly dug earth he indicated, last time, that she could use. Returns to the barn for tools along the path of beaten grass. Begins to mark out a row.

She stops digging and looks at the rows of vegetables in the neighbouring beds, all perfectly straight. By contrast, the trench she has made wavers. She goes back to her row and tries to even it up, mentally making a list of the things she will need—bamboo poles, string.

The soil smells slightly of iron, of leaves. Small stones appear occasionally but it has a lightness to it. It is not heavy and clayey, as the earth in her father's garden was. She opens a packet of bulbs—tulips—and looks at them in the dim daylight. It is three months past the optimum time to plant them. She bought them cheaply from a local discount store, but they look in good condition, a bright brown shiny sheath on the outside of the pure white bulb. Plant at twice the depth of bulb. She lays them out fifteen centimetres apart then covers them.

The beds are larger than she thought. She adds sawdust to the list in her head. In the next trench, she finds pieces of pottery, nondescript brown chunks which she lays to one side.

The last seeds she plants are poppies. Light, tiny, they are almost indistinguishable from the soil as soon as she sows them.

You've been busy. He stands by the side of the rabbit fence, an old oilskin over his suit.

Yes.

What have you been planting?

Bulbs, she says. Seeds. She fumbles for the packets and hands them to him. Her jeans are soaked from where she has been kneeling.

These are nice. He holds the empty poppy packet.

They were free. I wouldn't have bought them because the flowers don't last long. Only a day or so. But I can use the seed heads.

That's a shame. About the flowers.

Yes. It's often the way. The most beautiful don't last. Don't they?

Delphiniums. Poppies. Some of the most stunning garden roses shatter at a touch. So they're not so good for selling. I could use them for a wedding, or a funeral. It doesn't matter then.

What doesn't?

If they're only briefly at their best.

He is looking at her rows.

I should have made them straight. Next time I'll bring some string.

I've got some. Poles and string. Didn't you see them in the barn?

No.

The inside of the barn is crammed with stuff. Before he got ill, he tells her, he was a set designer. Now he works on the field. The quiet here, the growing things. It is his way of making himself better.

I found some pottery. While I was digging.

Ah. Can I see?

She hands him the lumps.

It's Roman, probably.

Really?

There are remains of an old Roman quay further down the valley by the creek. Other things: a bit of paving, a cist. I'll keep this. I'm making a collection of everything I dig up here. Everything that's uncovered. It's a kind of project. So, if you find anything else...

How do you tell? That it's Roman, I mean.

A friend of mine works at the museum. They analysed some pieces for me. The Romans were here for the tin and gold. And then there were the monks, from the old college at the head of the river. They used to grow food here. Some of the pottery is medieval.

Amazing.

Look, peregrine.

She does not want to look but, raising her head, she follows his finger to where the bird flies through veils of rain. She wants to know more about the Romans, the monks from the college so thoroughly destroyed few traces of it remain, aside from the odd gargoyle embedded in the neighbouring buildings; she wants to know about the other hands which worked this soil.

We should go in. Shelter from this. Do you want tea?

No, thanks. I'm soaked. She is cold now, having been still for so long. The thought of sitting in the caravan is not a pleasant one. I'll be back next week.

She collects up the seed packets, the bulb wrapper, her hand fork and trowel. Knocks mud off the spade and fork and carries them back to the barn. He opens the caravan door; warmth from the camp stove drifts out. Condensation fogs the windows. He is smiling at her, and she wonders what he is going to say.

Could you bring some milk when you come next time? I can't have dairy. Goat's milk. Or soya.

Sure, she says.

Back at the car she takes off her gumboots, her soaking coat, and loads them in the boot. Inside she strips off her jeans and wraps her lower half in a blanket. Drives home that way.

The next week she walks down the lane carrying two bags of bulbs. There are more varieties than she realised available; many of the flowers she used when she worked as a florist she can now begin to grow.

Out of the corner of her eye she sees him working in the far corner. From the top of the track, the land slopes as if it has been folded on the diagonal, all of it descending to the corner farthest from her. Because he is working near the bottom of the crease, it is hard to make out what he is doing.

She has forgotten the milk.

It has already started to bother her that it is his soil, his earth, his rules. That she is merely scratching, borrowing a few centimetres of surface. And yet she cannot imagine belonging to this place, it being hers. It is not what she would choose for herself. It is too high, too exposed. The jumbled boulders of the carn seem, at times, a reflection of her confusion. And then there is the cold, a deep earth-and-stone cold, the kind that gets in your bones. She wonders again what is wrong with him, what was wrong with him.

The quiet, though, also has a way of its own. In the way her life is away from this place, it feels like nourishment. Every action she initiates proceeds, un-thwarted, until it is complete. No one else to consider except for the too-thin man she sees out of the corner of her eye. She puts down her head and begins to dig.

She is planting *Liatris spicata*. The bulbs are dark, knobbly, a light hair of old, dried roots on their bases. Their hairiness reminds her of sea potatoes, found on the nearby beaches at low tide. When she looks up, she notices two parallel rows of bamboo canes, joined at their top apex, stand in one of the beds. Supports for what? Beans, perhaps, or peas. Everything he does out here, in the beds, is so neat. But it is not neat in the barn or in the caravan.

No rain today but it is cold. Smoky-yellow light crouches at the edges of the sky. February. Another row of bulbs: *Camassia leichtlinii*, a cultivar of quamash. The bulbs are white and smooth, small green shoots already sprouting from their apical points. It is far too late to be planting them. She tries and fails to think of May, when these bulbs will produce long straight green stems, and then star-shaped flowers, blue and cream.

She hears the soft sound of his boots on the grass. As she turns, reluctant to stop her work, she briefly wonders what he thinks of her. Her neck aches, so she rubs it.

More bulbs.

Yes. Look at these. She lifts an *Eremurus stenophyllus* tuber from brown paper, holding towards him the flat disc with its leggy roots, like the dried limbs of a once fleshy spider.

And they'll stay in the soil? Or will you lift them?

No. They'll stay. They form clumps. Bulbs like these, perennials, reproduce themselves asexually. Clone themselves, basically. So you get more flowers year on year.

This seems to surprise him. She has no idea what he knows or doesn't know about flowers.

Come and see the trees.

You're planting trees?

She follows him through the grass. Here, at the lowest point of the field, it is as sheltered from the wind as it is in the barn. The hedgerows are dense with the entwined stems of blackthorn, mayflower, holly. A few sloe berries glow dully purple black amongst bare thorns. The glossy green leaves and flowers of mature ivy pokes through the branches. Lifting her hand, removing her glove, she touches the odd, pale creamy globe.

This is the tree nursery.

Another bed won from the grass, enclosed by green windbreak that disappears, camouflaging its contents from the eye. Little tree whips, hundreds of them, two or three feet high and every one of them no more than a bare or sometimes branching twig. He says the name of a local valley, a secret place which runs down to the quiet waters of a forgotten creek.

I collected the seeds from the woods there. They've grown well. Oak. Beech. Ash. Hazel. Alder. As he names them, he touches the thin stems. He beckons and they walk higher up the slope. The grass is longer here, dead and white. This is where they'll be planted. Next weekend. I'm having a tree planting day. Can you come and help?

Yes, she says.

There'll be lots of people. All my friends.

Great, she says.

She is glad that he has friends. It counteracts the thought of him here, alone in his caravan, drinking from dirty cups, sleeping on a pile of damp blankets when she is home and warm.

There are already a lot of people at the field, she can tell by the cars on the lane. There is nowhere for her to park, so she drives back to the postbox and leaves her car there. As she walks back, she hears the gentle breath of horses in the field below the carn, sees the movement of their heads beyond the hedge, the tired planks of an old stable.

It takes her a while to find him. People talk to her, seem interested in what she is doing. They tell her things about the man who owns the field, assuming she knows more than she does; without her prompting his secrets spill out on the grass. They all seem excited by the fact that their friend has this surfeit of space. Many of them live on boats, in vans and caravans squeezed into corners of fields, fringes of towns and villages.

She sees him in the distance, reassesses his age down a notch and then down again. How much aged he is, whether by illness itself or the experience of illness, it is impossible to tell. It makes him more like her; it is the bridge that links her on one side and his friends on the other.

She has found out, quite recently, that her brother has been lying to her. For years, he has stolen from her, from the joint assets left to them by their parents. He calls what he did an act of love. It is not love. Away from here, her life is a shabby pile of documents, emails from lawyers and bank managers, statements of foreclosure, impending deadlines, dates for court. There is a chance that she will lose her house, lose everything she has worked for.

The friends start dragging dead wood into a circle. Someone sets light to it. Bottles appear, and a keg of beer. She plants *Nectaroscordum siculum*, an onion-paper fine sheath over its bulbs, which will one day be a handful of purple and green striped bells dangling from a wiggly stem. By the time she finishes, darkness is come. She looks over to the circle of light, sees his face, smiling. The flames give his face the colour it normally lacks; she catches a glimpse of how he must have looked and how he might, perhaps, one day look again.

In the weak sunlight, the green tips of the first bulbs she planted poke through the earth, cast tiny purple shadows on the soil. When she lifts her head, she sees what he has described to her, but she has never really believed. There is a view of the sea. Distant; complex with lines of trees and land in the foreground and further back, a skewed triangle of mint green water, a lilac sky.

The sunlight works on her back; from the damp sleeves of her jacket, steam rises. Tomorrow, February tips into March. In the soil she finds a lime green grub, curled and sleeping. More seeds have broken through the earth; tiny as watercress, they tremble as if exhausted by the division of their first leaf into two. She weeds around the green tips of the hyacinths; in some of their hearts, the flower spikes have already formed, are beginning to push upwards. She walks back to the car, returning with a bag of sawdust, light but bulky, cradled in her arms, and a carton of goat's milk in her pocket.

As she spreads the sawdust on the soil, the woody pine scent of it fills her throat. She walks to the barn and knocks on the caravan door. No reply. She opens it, leaving the milk on the floor where she hopes he will see it.

A cat comes and cries around her legs. She strokes it and it purrs. It is not fat, just well-furred, snug in its winter coat. She opens the door again. Cat biscuits and a bowl. The cat eats noisily. There is nothing to do but leave a note. She can write on the inside of a seed packet, but she has no pencil. She finds one on his table amongst textbooks and scientific books, most of them open, their pages marked with strips of paper. Beside them, a pad full of drawings and notes which she does not read.

I fed the cat. I hope it's yours. The goat's milk was fresh today 28/2. See you next week?

She leaves the note on the floor beside the milk. She is annoyed that she bought him milk and he isn't here. But she is also pleased. Words have stopped, are trapped inside her. She no longer trusts anyone. She does not want to talk. When she is here, she wants to plant flowers, row and rows of flowers, and wait and watch and tend them as they grow.

A violet beetle scuttles away under her hand. The *Triteleia laxa* goes in today, the sweet pea seeds, pre-scored. As she tries to unroll the chicken wire mesh she bought to support the plants, she realises she needs help.

Before she interrupted him, he was using wooden pallets to construct a series of compost heaps. Earlier he was planting comfrey plants in nice, straight rows. She has tried the string and bamboo method but her rows are never straight. She has gone back to working by eye. The poppies and the cornflowers are through. The love-lies-bleeding. The soil is warming. The irises have produced grey, strap-fine leaves.

Which kinds of flowers are edible?

Violets, marigolds, nasturtiums, day lilies, she tells him. Borage flowers, courgette flowers. The petals of Sweet William, apple blossom, sunflower and rose. Cornflower, lavender, pansies. Bergamot. Evening primrose.

As they are talking, a change comes over him.

I must go and lie down.

He is burying something. An animal he found on the road. He shows her a new area above where the trees are planted which will be a cemetery. And then he says that there is a car buried lower down the field.

You buried a car?

Yes.

Why?

My friend drove it up here and then it broke down. He didn't want it anymore and I didn't want to pay to have it towed away. Come and look.

Down by the hedge, he pulls back some long grass, exposing the back window of a hatchback. He wipes the window, but the interior is dark. He peers inside as if he expects to see something in there. She does not like looking at the window, does not like the thought of its dark interior. What sort of person buries a car?

As they are walking back to the flowerbeds, he says, Thank you for the milk.

I didn't bring any today.

Never mind.

Another time I was here, she says, there was a cat. Is it your cat?

The cat is an outlaw. There are signs up, offering a reward for his return, down in the village. I could do with the money, but I'm not going to turn him in. He seems to like it here.

She can understand why the cat likes it here. It is a good place to be a cat.

What are you planting?

Lavender. She has bought plug plants and potted them on, hardened them off in her courtyard garden. Against the vastness of the field, they seem tiny. She plants them through a layer of weed matting, cutting crosses and slotting one plant into each gap.

How long will they last for?

They'll grow and get bigger for about ten years. And then they'll die.

Her father had edged their rose beds with French lavender, to keep the aphids off, but the plants had struggled in the clayey soil, had never thrived. These are a different type, an English lavender, a pale blue simple flower good for cutting and to use in cooking, the dried flower for repelling insects, fragrancing clothes, as an aid to sleep.

From a packet he spills red and white seeds, shiny and marbled like Florentine paper, into his palm.

Beans and peas enrich the soil, she says. They fix nitrogen. When I was at school, we dug up the roots of a gorse bush, cut open the white nodules growing on them—inside was this blood-like stuff. Like haemoglobin, apparently. I've been fond of gorse ever since.

Someone gave a gorse flower remedy to me. When I was in hospital.

Did it help?

I don't know. Maybe.

She thinks he has finished talking but then he says, It's supposed to be for those who have given up hope. Or lost their belief.

The day is ending. She hears the sound of cars, footsteps and voices echoing down the track, the clink of bottles. The friends replenish the fire with new, dry boughs. He tries to keep working but the friends distract him, keep him busy, talking. In the fading light he shifts from old to young, young to old.

Her back aches. She tidies her things and looks at what she has achieved. There is very little to be seen; the bulk of her labour lies beneath the darkening surface of the soil.

Above her head the sky has turned the serious kind of blue that means that darkness is not far away. Someone lights the fire. Through the still air, she hears the sharp crackle of flames and smells dry wood burning.

Today she plants the last of the bulbs, all alliums, long-lasting tall-stemmed purple globes in various shapes and sizes. An idea, a comment, a question, a friend of a friend—all of these things have led her here. Now the hyacinths are on the cusp of flowering.

He has also been planning and planting. She has helped him to lift off the turf and peel it back, in preparation for a second row of beds.

As the soil warms the weeds have started to grow; the perennial buttercup, its net-like roots spread horizontally, is particularly hard to shift. The white roots of dandelions, zigzags of light in the dark soil, their wounds leaking a milky sap.

She had feared that the flowers might not bloom

when they were supposed to, because of her lateness in planting them, the height of the land, the subsequent cold. And the wind has been easterly and northerly, bringing snow winds from the Arctic, rather than the prevailing warm and damp south-westerly. Even on a bright day like today, her ears ring with cold and, inside gloves, the tips of her fingers are numb. As she cuts through the thick, sappy stems of the hyacinths, washes the dirt off the leaves and lower flowers, the few open bells release a clean, sweet scent.

He digs for a while and then he stops and coughs. Whatever is wrong with him is taking its time to give up its hold. The damp caravan can only be making things worse. She wants to drag it out of the barn and into the sun, open the doors, let the whole thing heat up, dry out. There is something about this place. You could retreat here, curl up in damp blankets and bury yourself in its silence, its various winds, its swaying grasses. Sink into it and be covered by it, as the car has been covered by earth and grass.

He has gone to drink water, hand resting on the tap until the coughing eases. His clothes still hang on him like the clothes on a scarecrow. When was he last well? When did he last live in a house? This coldness rising from the earth she considers his enemy. She thinks he does not do enough to protect himself against it. How can he become better if he is not warm? How will he get better if he drinks from filthy mugs?

He has seen her looking at him and now he beckons her. She climbs over the fence, her shoulders tense.

He points to a new ridge of earth by the side of the barn. From here she can see thin sticks are planted in it.

Willows, he says.
They'll grow big.
I know.
Why here?
Because this is where the house will go.
You're building a house?
One day.
To live in?
Isn't that why most people build houses?
I thought...But she doesn't know what she had thought.
I thought you knew.
I didn't know.
He begins talking about dwelling rights, planning permission. He plans to build a house out of straw bales, with wool as insulation. He has been collecting the materials in the barn, most of which are free or recycled, to build his house of straw.

She cuts the *Camassia leichtlinii 'Alba'*, secures five stems with a rubber band and drops them in a bucket. The alliums are ready, the tall types called Gladiator and Purple Sensation, the shorter lavender starburst of *Allium christophii*. Once they are all cut and bunched, she moves them into the shade. The sun is higher in the sky; the breeze is light and warm. Small birds, hidden by bud-covered branches, sing.
He is digging in the lower field. A deep, narrow hole.
What are you trying to find?
Water. I just don't know how deep it is.
How do you know it's here?
I had a dowser come. The twigs twitched.
When rain had driven him in from the garden, her

father used to stand at the window and watch it fall. Nothing exists without water, he'd say.

She passes him a length of wood and he uses it to brace the side of the hole against collapse. The soil darkens the deeper he goes. Chunks of rock protrude from the shaft walls.

Someone is walking towards them, over the grass, hidden behind the light. Because she has been thinking of her father, it is him she sees until she blinks, once, twice and the image recedes. It is one of the friends, come to help. The friend is not tall, but he has substance. He does not say much, just extends his arm into the hole to help the man who owns the field out and then climbs in himself.

Dahlia tubers lie in the trench like a row of shrivelled sweet potato. She covers them and then plants sedum around the edges of the bed, a type with purple-black leaves and, come September, small, hard, ruby flowers.

She is beginning to realise that he did not think she would plant anything permanent. He expected that she would grow flowers from seed and harvest them, an annual crop. It would be possible, though it would severely limit the range of flowers. There would be little for her to do for much of the year.

There has been this miscommunication, right from the beginning. It is probably the result of her reluctance to talk, her failure to realise that he did not know much about flowers, his assumption that they were grown in the same way as vegetables.

She tells herself it does not matter. Everything she plants can be dug up again and moved. Like people, flowers travel: transplanted with care, they usually managed to re-establish themselves, to put down new roots.

She is ready to go. She walks over to the shaft. He sits on the edge with his legs dangling into the hole. His friend is below, pickaxing lumps of earth into a bucket.

Goodbye, she says to them.

Goodbye, he says. Can you bring some milk next time?

The shaft is very deep now, but there is still no water. She doesn't like it, wishes he would fill it in or cover it. A mound of spoil lies next to it. When she gives him the milk, he tells her he plans to get a digger in, to grade the earth where the house will go and to scoop out a pond.

In the sunlight he seems brighter, better defined. Not well, exactly, but strengthening. He is still too thin. Sometimes he lies and sleeps on the grass in the sunlight. It makes her think of childhood, the heat of long-ago sun, the smell of grass rich in her nose, the ozone scent of the summer harbour.

Life holds no story unless that story is the growing and the dying. Twice in her life she has tried to run away from flowers, the first time from her family's floristry business where she worked every day after school, at weekends and in holidays, and the second time when, during the last recession, out of financial necessity, she worked as a florist in London. Yet here she is, back among them. They follow her, it seems. Or she, unwittingly, unwillingly, follows them. They present themselves to her as opportunities, the only options. With them she feels entirely comfortable, as if they were part of her, were members of her family. She knows their common and Latin names; some have been her companions since earliest childhood, their names learnt alongside her own; they have always been amongst the most important inhabitants of her world. The flowers she grows, that line up wonkily behind her back like a beautiful army, are not as delicate as they look. They are all survivors.

The grass in the far field lengthens, its gold touched with pink. Everywhere there is blossom and red campion, Queen Anne's Lace with its scarlet drop of blood. In the shade, the furry leaves of foxgloves hold the dew until the morning's shadows burn away into midday.

I brought you some milk, she says.

Come and see the pond, he says.

Below the flower beds, a digger has scraped out a shallow basin in the earth, tipping the excess soil at the far edge, building it up into a bank. The effect is pleasing, as if the far lip of the pond were somehow floating above the lower parts of the field.

In her childhood garden, there was a stream, dividing the formal beds around the house from the secret spaces of a stand of native bush. A simple bridge, arch-backed, connected the two worlds; she remembers what it was to paddle in that stream, the little beach of pale gold gravel it left before it exited the property, edged by a rustling screen of bamboo.

So water, yes.

Nothing exists without water.

Last time she was here, he was dragging straw bales out of the barn with scrawny arms. Already the house has walls and spaces for doors and windows. She cannot see him; assuming he is still asleep, she walks into the space the straw encloses and holds out her hands.

So many things are flowering: the *Liatris spicata*, the *Triteleia laxa*, the *Eryngium planum*, gladioli, nigella, cornflowers, sweet peas. Her time now is taken up with cutting and bunching, weeding and covering the soil in mulch to stop it losing moisture to the sun. It is too hot now to work beyond midday; she comes early to cut the flowers, weeds a little, leaves by eleven or twelve.

He is often asleep when she arrives, only rising when she is about to go. When she hears the caravan door open, she looks up, expecting to see him, but a woman comes out and walks towards the standpipe to fill the kettle.

Hello.

Who are you? the woman says.

I'm the one who grows the flowers.

He comes out of the caravan, rubbing his hair. Lifting his tee-shirt, he scratches his stomach.

Can you give Sally a lift back to town? When you're finished, he says. Are you finished?

Yes. Pretty much. Just tidying up.

But we haven't had breakfast yet, Sally says. I haven't even had a cup of tea.

You can have breakfast when you get home.

Are you trying to get rid of me, Sally says, before I've had a cup of tea?

Of course not, he says. I'll make you some tea. Would you like tea, too?

No thanks, she says. I'm going soon. But I brought some milk.

As she carries the flowers back and forth to the edge of the track, Sally sits on one of the benches by the fire circle and talks to her. The things Sally says are funny in a pithy kind of way. She's pretty, too.

He brings out two mugs of tea.

I'm off now.

Do you mind giving Sally a lift?

Not at all.

I think I'll spend the day here, Sally says, stretching and looking around. It's going to be a beautiful day.

Do what you like, he says. But you should know that I've got work to do.

Don't mind me. Sally lies back on the boards, folding her hands over her stomach, shutting her eyes. I'll be just fine.

After some weeks of summer rain, the pond is filling up; the water is pale bronze, the suspended particles of soil in it yet to settle. He is thigh deep in the water, planting marginals on a shelf a foot or so below the surface. The scent of water is softly mineral, a note of freshness amongst the dry summer scents of dust and grass.

Flower buds form on the tiny lavender bushes; the red leaves of the sedum are dark as wine; the dahlias, already three feet tall, release their peculiar smell as she brushes past them. For most of her life she has thought of them, wrongly, as South African. But they are Mexican, a plant whose tubers must be lifted in October so that they do not rot.

What is winter underneath this sun? Its memory lies in the earth, beneath the bark of the shrubs, the trees. It lies in leaves which lift their faces to the light. It lies in the pollen, gold and grey, the bees collect and carry with them from flower to flower.

The martagon lilies are four feet tall, whorls of leaves wrapping their stems like deep green ruffs, their pale purple flowers recurved.

When she looks over to the pond, she sees him floating on his back, arms and legs splayed out, five-pointed as a fallen star.

Years later, at the end, when it's time to move on, she

drives down the track for the last time to dig up and move the last of the flowers. She does not see him. He is not there, Sally tells her. He has gone to work in Greece for a while. A project. Sustainable building.

Sally stands in the doorway of the house made of straw. I've got a flat in a proper house again, she says, so I'll be moving on too.

The wool they'd used as insulation had been full of moth larvae. They'd had a massive infestation, as well as trouble with mice.

What sort of trouble with mice?

They were falling out of the ceiling onto my face, Sally says, while I was asleep.

What's the solution?

Sally shrugs. Perhaps the moths have got into the straw. Perhaps the house will have to be torn down, and they'll start again somehow. He's gone away to get some experience of building the kind of place he wants here, and to have time to think.

Time to think. She had had it in the hours that she spent here on her knees, eyes on the ground, hands in the good earth.

The trees, grown from seed, are taller than her now. The bulbs she planted have multiplied, the lavenders filled out from tiny plugs to dense, thick pads. She will not move the lavenders; they will remain along with some other things that are difficult to shift. Though she tries to be thorough and lift them carefully, she is bound to miss some bulbs. After she is gone, they will put up their heads each spring, aiming for the light.

The flowers she leaves behind. Will he think of them as a nuisance?

Or a gift?

She is moving. To a house with a garden big enough

to hold these flowers. It is necessary to have them always with her, not to be separated from them, even by the distance of a few miles.

Time to say goodbye.

She walks around the property and, finally, over to the pond. On its green-grey surface water lilies float, white and cream and copper-red. Sedge and flag iris soften the margins of the pool. The reflection of the sky and the clouds is on the water, and in the pull between the horizontal and vertical lines she feels it, as she felt it when she was a child, a sense of dissolution between here and now and whatever lies just out of reach.

Here.

Whatever has filtered down into the darkness has given life to flowers which open like a hand; in the centre of each a deepening of colour, which she can hear as if it were a sound.

Nothing exists without water.

She thinks of him and knows that he is well.

Notes

Three Roads contains stories written over the last nine years. Some have been published previously, in print and online.

'A Bird So Rare' was first published in *takahē 84* and subsequently in *Over the Dam* and *Cornish Short Stories: A Collection of Contemporary Cornish Writing* in 2018.

A shorter version of 'Flowers' was first published in the Bristol Short Story Prize Anthology 8 (Tangent Publishing: Bristol, 2015). It was Seren Short Story of the Month in March 2019 and Fairlight Books Short Story of the Week on 6 May 2021.

'Girls on Motorbikes' was commended in the Prolitzer Prize for Prose Writing, 2015.

'Impressionism' was first published in *Meniscus*, the online journal of the Australasian Association of Writing Programs (AAWP), Volume 5, Issue 1, 2017.

'La Crue de la Seine' was first published on the *Ink, Sweat and Tears* webzine in 2016 and subsequently in *Elbow Room*, Volume 16, 2017. Another version was included in *Bonsai: The Big Book of Small Stories* (Canterbury University Press: Christchurch, New Zealand, 2018). It was inspired by letters Katherine Mansfield wrote while staying at 13 Quai des Fleurs, Paris in 1915. During my own first visit to the city in 2014, I dreamt that Paris was inundated by a vast flood. I later heard that the city's motto is *Fluctuat nec mergitut—It is tossed by waves but does not sink.*

'Over the Dam' won the Sara Park Memorial Short Story Competition in 2013 and was published in the pamphlet *Over the Dam*.

'Peregian' was first published in *Over the Dam*, (Red Squirrel Press, 2015).

'Stars', one of the winning entries in the Solstice Shorts Festival Competition 2014, was published in *Solstice Shorts: Sixteen Stories about Time* (Arachne Press: London, 2015).

'The Rememberer' was first published in *The Interpreter's House 55*, March 2014 and subsequently in *Over the Dam*.

'Tissue' was published as one of a series of postcards to celebrate Elbow Room's fifth birthday in July 2017.

Acknowledgements

Sincere thanks to Sheila Wakefield, Founder Editor of Red Squirrel Press, and Colin Will, Editor of Postbox Press, the fiction imprint of Red Squirrel Press, for publishing this book. Many thanks also to Gerry Cambridge for the beautiful typesetting & design.

Three Roads was written with the support of the Complete MS Programme run by the New Zealand Society of Authors Te Puni Kaitahu O Aotearoa (PEN NZ Inc) and funded by Creative New Zealand.

Thank you to Helen Chaloner, Michelle Phillips and Heather Holcroft-Pinn at Literature Works, the regional development body for literature in South West England, for supporting my writing in many ways.

My gratitude to the following writers, editors and publishers who have critiqued, selected and published these stories: Majella Cullinane; Helen Ivory; Sheila Wakefield, Ellen Phethean and Kathleen Kenny; Cherry Potts, Anita Sethi, Alison Moore, Robert Shearman and Imogen Robertson; Martin Malone; Karen Zelas, Cassandra Fusco and all at *takahē*; Joe Melia, Nikesh Shukla, Sara Davies, Rowan Lawton and Sanjida O'Connell; Jaki McCarrick; Rosie Sherwood and Zelda Chappell; Paul Hetherington, Jen Webb, Gail Pittaway and Shane Strange; Frankie McMillan, James Norcliffe and Michelle Elvy; and Elou Carroll.

Thank you to Lindsay Bennett-Ford, Maria Donovan, Emily Duncan and Stefan Lane, Clare Howdle, Sarah Jane Humphrey, Carole Inman, Sue Kittow, Candy Neubert, Felicity Notley, Becky Tipper, Hils Tranter and Sue Wells for kind words of encouragement.

As always, I would like to thank Adam, Iris and Lauren Drouet for their constancy and understanding. This book is for them.

A NOTE ON THE TYPES

The text of this book is set in Palatino Nova Pro,
Hermann Zapf's & Akira Koyabashi's redesign
& updating in several weights
of Zapf's classic Palatino, which was originally
released in 1950. Renowned for its legibility,
it takes its name from Giambattista Palatino,
a calligraphy master & contemporary of Da Vinci.

Titles are set in the companion face Palatino Sans,
Zapf & Koyabashi's curved and rounded sans
serif designed as a contemporary
complement to its classic precursor.